"You and me—

Quinn muttered, fighting the need to pull Victoria into his arms.

"Why isn't this a good idea?" she asked, her voice a husky murmur in the hushed, expectant silence of the room.

"Because you're a safe, settled woman. And I'm not the boy next door."

"What makes you think I want the boy next door? Maybe I like dangerous men."

The grip of callused fingers tightened reflexively, his thumb stroked across soft cotton and found silky skin. His gaze flickered to her mouth and downward to her throat.

"Not a good idea," he murmured, distracted by the contrast of his work-roughened fingers, dark against her pale skin. "A woman is likely to lose her good reputation—and a lot more. This won't work, Victoria. Find yourself a nice, safe man—and forget this happened."

Dear Reader,

Happy 20th Anniversary, Silhouette! And Happy Valentine's Day to all! There are so many ways to celebrate…starting with six spectacular novels this month from Special Edition.

Reader favorite Joan Elliott Pickart concludes Silhouette's exciting cross-line continuity ROYALLY WED with *Man…Mercenary… Monarch,* in which a beautiful woman challenges a long-lost prince to give up his loner ways.

In *Dr. Mom and the Millionaire,* Christine Flynn's latest contribution to the popular series PRESCRIPTION: MARRIAGE, a marriage-shy tycoon suddenly experiences a sizzling attraction—to his gorgeous doctor! And don't miss the next SO MANY BABIES—in *Who's That Baby?* by Diana Whitney, an infant girl is left on a Native American attorney's doorstep, and he turns to a lovely pediatrician for help.…

Next is Lois Faye Dyer's riveting *Cattleman's Courtship,* in which a brooding, hard-hearted rancher is undeniably drawn to a chaste, sophisticated lady. And in Sharon De Vita's provocative family saga, THE BLACKWELL BROTHERS, tempers—and passions— flare when a handsome Apache man offers *The Marriage Basket* to a captivating city gal.

Finally, you'll be swept up in the drama of Trisha Alexander's *Falling for an Older Man,* another tale in the CALLAHANS & KIN series, when an unexpected night of passion leaves Sheila Callahan with a nine-month secret.

So, curl up with a Special Edition novel and celebrate this Valentine's Day with thoughts of love and happy dreams of forever!

Happy reading,

Karen Taylor Richman,
Senior Editor

Please address questions and book requests to:
Silhouette Reader Service
U.S.: 3010 Walden Ave., P.O. Box 1325, Buffalo, NY 14269
Canadian: P.O. Box 609, Fort Erie, Ont. L2A 5X3

LOIS FAYE DYER

CATTLEMAN'S COURTSHIP

Silhouette®

SPECIAL ▼ **EDITION**®

Published by Silhouette Books

America's Publisher of Contemporary Romance

For all the romance readers at Paperbacks Plus
in Port Orchard, Washington, especially Joanne, Nikki,
Renate, Sheila and Susan B.

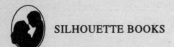 SILHOUETTE BOOKS

ISBN 0-373-24306-5

CATTLEMAN'S COURTSHIP

Copyright © 2000 by Lois Faye Dyer

This edition published by arrangement with Harlequin Books S.A.

Visit us at www.romance.net

Printed in U.S.A.

Books by Lois Faye Dyer

Silhouette Special Edition

Lonesome Cowboy #1038
He's Got His Daddy's Eyes #1129
The Cowboy Takes a Wife #1198
The Only Cowboy for Caitlin #1253
Cattleman's Courtship #1306

LOIS FAYE DYER,

winner of the 1989-1990 *Romantic Times Magazine*
Reviewer's Choice Award for Best New Series Author,
lives on Washington State's beautiful Puget Sound with
her husband and their yellow Lab, Maggie Mae. She
ended a career as a paralegal and Superior Court clerk to
fulfill a lifelong dream to write. When she's not involved
in writing, she enjoys long walks on the beach with her
husband, watching musical and Western movies from
the 1940s and 1950s, and, most of all, indulging her
passionate addiction to reading. This is her twelfth
published novel.

IT'S OUR 20th ANNIVERSARY!
We'll be celebrating all year,
continuing with these fabulous titles,
on sale in February 2000.

Special Edition

**#1303 Man...Mercenary...
Monarch**
Joan Elliott Pickart

**#1304 Dr. Mom and the
Millionaire**
Christine Flynn

#1305 Who's That Baby?
Diana Whitney

**#1306 Cattleman's
Courtship**
Lois Faye Dyer

#1307 The Marriage Basket
Sharon De Vita

#1308 Falling for an Older Man
Trisha Alexander

Intimate Moments

**#985 The Wildes of
Wyoming—Chance**
Ruth Langan

#986 Wild Ways
Naomi Horton

#987 Mistaken Identity
Merline Lovelace

#988 Family on the Run
Margaret Watson

#989 On Dangerous Ground
Maggie Price

#990 Catch Me If You Can
Nina Bruhns

Romance

VIRGIN BRIDES

**#1426 Waiting for the
Wedding**
Carla Cassidy

BREWSTER
BABY BOOM

#1427 Bringing Up Babies
Susan Meier

#1428 The Family Diamond
Moyra Tarling

The WEDDING
AUCTION

**#1429 Simon Says...Marry
Me!**
Myrna Mackenzie

**#1430 The Double Heart
Ranch**
Leanna Wilson

#1431 If the Ring Fits...
Melissa McClone

Desire

MAN
OF THE
MONTH

**#1273 A Bride for Jackson
Powers**
Dixie Browning

#1274 Sheikh's Temptation
Alexandra Sellers

#1275 The Daddy Salute
Maureen Child

#1276 Husband for Keeps
Kate Little

#1277 The Magnificent M.D.
Carol Grace

#1278 Jesse Hawk: Brave Father
Sheri WhiteFeather

Chapter One

The Crossroads Bar and Grill was loud and rowdy when Quinn Bowdrie stepped through the archway, undecided if he wanted to stay or head home to the comfort of his bed. He leaned the point of one broad shoulder against the wall just inside the door, thumbs hooked in his belt, hands hanging idly while he looked over the Saturday night crowd. He didn't see the blonde he'd noticed entering the bar earlier, but the room was packed with townspeople from Colson and ranchers from surrounding spreads. When he'd first seen her, he'd been tempted to push out of the

Grill's booth and follow her for a closer look, but the mouthwatering aroma of steak and baked potato had reminded him that he hadn't eaten since noon.

Although Quinn often ate a meal at the Grill, he rarely socialized with his neighbors at the popular attached bar. Nevertheless, he decided to go next door to look for the blonde after he finished his dinner.

The throng parted briefly, allowing him a glimpse of a familiar face on the far side of the room. Nikki Peterson's auburn hair was a blaze of color beneath the bar's low-wattage lights. She'd been actively pursuing his brother, Cully, for a good two months. But as far as Quinn was aware, his brother considered her strictly a friend. There were times Quinn envied his brother's ability to enjoy women. Quinn himself had decided long ago that anything more involved than a rare one-night stand wasn't worth the effort.

The crowd shifted again, allowing a clear view of the woman who sat across from Nikki. She laughed and shook her head at something Nikki said, and the dim light glittered off the silvery fall of hair that hung just past her shoulders. There was an innate sensuality in her movements, and Quinn's eyes narrowed as he continued to watch her, his attention riveted as everything male in him responded to the subtle female signals she was sending. She turned slightly to answer Nikki, and light fell over her face.

Quinn stiffened and pushed away from the wall, his hands loosening their grip and sliding unnoticed from his belt. He couldn't tell what color her eyes were from this distance and the dim light only gave a hint of a lush mouth and finely molded cheekbones, but it was enough to make him want to see more.

His gaze slid lower, following the silvery hair where it fell across her shoulders, shimmering like pale silk against the soft peach of her blouse. The edge of the tabletop kept him from seeing all of her, but what he could observe of her aroused an insatiable need to view the rest of her. Unfortunately, his view was blocked when a man paused at the table. A brief moment later, the man held out his hand and the woman rose reluctantly from the booth, walking onto the dance floor, the man turning to follow her.

Quinn all but snarled. Sam Beckman was a local rancher with a reputation for playing fast and loose with women. The pretty blonde was going to get hit on, hard.

Hell, he thought with disgust. As pretty as she is, she's probably used to men coming on to her.

Common sense told him to go home but the

sight of the woman dancing with Beckman made him stay. Quinn leaned against the wall, stuck his hands into his front pockets and watched Sam and the stranger.

The music was fast and loud. Sam expertly swung the woman through a series of intricate steps, and she followed him with smooth ease. The dim light on the dance floor gleamed off her silvery hair as she spun and shifted, her lush mouth curved in laughter as she ducked beneath Sam's arm and twirled away again. The song ended; without pausing, the band moved smoothly into a slow, bluesy tune, and Sam pulled his partner into his arms.

Quinn's gaze followed the couple as the rancher slow-stepped the blonde across the crowded dance floor toward the darkest corner of the room, the one closest to Quinn. His eyes narrowed, his body tensed as he watched the pretty stranger plant her hand against Beckman's shoulder and push in an attempt to put space between them. Beckman resisted and forced her closer, bending his head to whisper in her ear. Quinn's irritation moved a notch higher. The woman stopped dancing and pushed away from Sam, the frown on her face leaving no doubt that she wasn't enticed by whatever he'd whispered in her ear.

She hadn't gone two steps away from him when Beckman, laughing, reached out and caught her arm, pulling her back into his grasp.

That does it, Quinn decided grimly. He shoved away from the wall and strode onto the dance floor. It took only a few short seconds to reach the couple and tap Beckman on the shoulder.

"What the..."

"I'm cutting in."

Beckman's surprise turned into annoyance. "Sorry, Quinn. I saw her first." His hand tightened possessively around her arm.

Quinn contemplated slugging the vain rancher on his picture-perfect jaw. He glanced at the woman and jerked at the heat that surged through his veins. She was even prettier up close. Her eyes were deep blue and snapping with anger. Quinn forgot what he'd meant to say to her. Fortunately, she wasn't struck speechless.

"I'm not a piece of merchandise."

The husky, annoyed feminine tone feathered shivers of awareness up Quinn's spine.

"I didn't..." Beckman protested.

Quinn and the blonde ignored him.

"Do you want to dance with me or him?" He asked, his gaze holding hers.

"You."

He held out his hand and she placed hers in his,

palm to palm, and his fingers threaded possessively between hers. It wasn't until he tugged
gently and she stepped toward him that they realized Sam Beckman still had his hand wrapped
around her forearm.

Quinn turned his head, and his gaze pinned
Beckman's. "Let go of her," he said softly. His
tone was lethal.

Beckman's gaze flicked from Quinn to the
blonde and back again before he glowered and
released her. "Hell, Quinn," he said truculently.
"I didn't even know you could dance."

"I can dance." Quinn didn't bother adding that
he rarely practiced the social skill an old friend
had taught him. He stared at Beckman for a full
minute before the rancher shrugged, muttered under his breath, turned on his heel and left.

Victoria Denning barely noticed when Sam
Beckman left. She was far too busy staring at the
man holding her hand. He was at least six feet
tall, with broad, muscle-layered shoulders. The
pearl snaps of his white cotton dress shirt were
unfastened at the throat, the cuffs of the long
sleeves rolled up to bare powerful forearms
dusted with fine black hair. Faded denim jeans
outlined muscled thighs and long legs; black cowboy boots covered his feet. He had a straight blade
of a nose and high cheekbones; his mouth was

thin-lipped and hard. His hair was black as a raven's wing, and sea-green eyes inspected her from beneath black brows.

Quinn read the same fascinated attraction in the woman's blue eyes that was hitting him in subtly erotic waves. Every male hormone in his body was on alert, as he responded to a body that was seductively curved and the subtle scent of perfume and warm woman.

Someone bumped him, and Quinn glanced behind him. Only then did he realize that he was standing still, staring at her, while all around them, couples swayed together to the music. He smiled wryly.

Victoria caught her breath and forgot to exhale. The brief curving of his lips softened the austere, hard-boned lines of his face into heart-stopping handsomeness.

"I guess we should dance." He tugged her closer and slipped an arm around her waist, moving her easily to the slow rhythm of the music.

Being held in the loose circle of his arms was like being encircled by live electrical wires. He turned her, his thigh brushing briefly against hers, and a shiver of awareness chased over her skin.

"Thanks for rescuing me." She smiled up at him. "I'm Victoria Denning."

"Quinn Bowdrie," he answered. "You must

be new in town—didn't anyone warn you about Beckman?''

"That he was an octopus?" she asked. His mouth tilted in a swift half smile. Once again she felt the kick of pure adrenaline rushing through her veins. "No, no one warned me. But then, no one told me that Colson has a resident white knight named Quinn, either.''

He shot her a quick, disbelieving glance.

"A white knight?" He shook his head firmly. "Not me, lady. That's the last thing anybody would ever tell you about me."

"Really?" She tipped her head back and indulged her need to look at him. The shadows in the dark corner of the dance floor were broken by the flickering reflections of colored light from the mirrored globe hung in the center of the ceiling. The uneven light alternately illuminated and darkened his features. "Why not?"

"You really are new in town, aren't you? Wait a while," he said brusquely. "You'll find out."

"Why don't you tell me—then I won't have to wait."

Quinn briefly thought about telling her the truth—that Quinn Bowdrie wasn't considered fit company for a lady. Especially not one who looked and smelled as well-cared for as she did.

Especially not one who heated his blood just by smiling at him.

Instead he decided to skirt the truth and buy himself a little time and a few more stolen moments of holding her in his arms, even if the chaste and proper distance he kept between them was killing him.

"No. I think I'll let you find out on your own. I've never had a woman call me a white knight," he drawled easily. "I think I'd like to enjoy it for a while."

She laughed, the sound a low, throaty chuckle that eased over his skin like a caress.

"Hmm. A mystery man." Victoria glanced up at him, and her breath lodged in her throat. The muscled arm circling her waist had slowly tightened until her body just brushed his as they swayed to the slow beat. Each breath she took drew in the faint, clean aroma of soap and spicy aftershave. Victoria was accustomed to men looking at her with interest, but the undisguised male heat deep in Quinn's eyes made her skin tighten and warm. Her nerves shivered with awareness, all her senses on overload, and she searched for something to diffuse the charged silence. "It's true that you're not wearing a suit of armor—I'm guessing by your clothes that you're not a storekeeper, either."

"Nope."

"Hmm. Maybe a rancher?"

"How did you guess?"

His expression was solemnly surprised, but his green eyes lit with amusement.

"It might have been the jeans and pearl-snapped Western shirt," she answered. "But the real giveaway was the cowboy boots."

"Uh-oh." He glanced at his feet. "Corral dirt and hay on the soles?"

Victoria's gaze took in the polished but worn black leather.

"No. Unlike boots worn by cowboys in Seattle, yours actually look like you wear them regularly."

"Seattle? Is that where you live?"

"Yes. Until a week ago. I'm staying with my aunt and uncle temporarily. But as soon as I find an apartment to rent, I'll be an official resident of Colson."

"No kidding? What brought you to Colson?"

"Allergies," Victoria answered, her voice husky from the effort to breathe normally when he turned her smoothly to the music, his thigh sliding briefly against hers. She lifted her gaze to his and found she couldn't look away. The sound of the music and the crowd around them faded. At the advanced age of twenty-seven, after the usual round of dating and one semiserious involvement during college, Victoria found herself confronted for the first time by an overwhelming, mind-scrambling, female reaction to a male. Her skin felt flushed; her heart was beating twice its normal rate; her breath came faster as she took short, shallow breaths and with each inhalation, drew in the distinctly male scent of aftershave warmed by body heat.

"Allergies?" Quinn said disbelievingly. He took a slow, thorough inventory of her body from the top of her silky head to her small feet. "That's hard to believe. I've never seen anyone who looked healthier."

Victoria, who had perfected the art of squelching interested males with one well-aimed, frigid stare, felt his sea-green gaze stroke over her as if he'd brushed his hand up and down her body and realized with amazement that she was blushing like a teenager.

"Thank you, but unfortunately, it's true," she managed to get out. "I have severe allergies."

"Really? To what?"

"Almost everything that grows in and around Seattle," she answered promptly, "especially pine trees and Scotch broom."

"What's a Scotch broom?" Quinn asked. He didn't really care, but he wanted to keep her talking. The slightly husky tones of her voice feathered over his skin in soft, enticing strokes.

"It's not a real broom," she laughed, her blue eyes lighting with amusement. "It's a plant."

"Then why do they call it a broom?" he asked, bemused by the way her whole face lit up when she smiled.

"I have no idea. It was planted along the Washington State highways years ago. It spread like wildfire and now, every spring when it blooms, thousands of allergy sufferers, like me, are absolutely miserable."

"Well, we don't have Scotch broom here, so you should be safe," he commented. "At least from the plant life."

His mouth tilted in a lazy grin while his gaze moved slowly over her face to fasten intently on her mouth. That hot green stare returned to meet hers with such blatant intent that Victoria caught her breath.

She didn't doubt for a minute that he was dangerous. Not to mention the fact that he was clearly a cowboy, and she'd learned not to trust the breed during summers spent in Colson as a teenager. But being held close to him was so exhilarating that her blood fizzed as if she'd had an infusion of champagne bubbles. She hated the lack of control over her life that her health had forced her to accept. She'd opted for serious and *safe* all her life; suddenly she was tired of safe and sane. Besides, even her cousin, Lonna, had told her she needed to lighten up and learn to have fun.

So when Quinn's arm tightened a fraction, gently urging her closer, Victoria allowed it, giving in to the need to feel the heat of his body against hers. She'd never thought of herself as a particularly sensual woman, but Quinn stirred and heightened an awareness of her own body and an irresistible curiosity for the feel of his that she couldn't deny.

He tucked her close, his cheek resting lightly against her hair, his breath gently stirring the silky strands.

"Maybe someone should warn you away from the animal life in Colson."

His voice was a husky murmur of sound in her ear. Victoria shivered with awareness.

"What kind of animal life?"

"Beckman, for one."

"Oh."

"If you were dancing with him in this dark corner, he'd be kissing you by now."

"Ah. But I'm not dancing with Mr. Beckman," she said lightly, trying to ignore the heavy thud of her heart and the press of his chest against her breasts, the heavy muscles of his thighs flexing smoothly against hers as they swayed together. "I'm dancing with you."

"That's not exactly safe, either."

"Really? Why?"

He turned his head and close-shaven though he was, still she felt the slight rasp of masculine, beard-roughened skin against her cheek.

"Because I'm having a lot of trouble remembering why I shouldn't be kissing you myself." He said bluntly.

Victoria's nerves jumped. "Oh?" She turned her cheek and found his lips a whisper from hers. Bewildered by the breathless, hot reaction that swept her, she wondered dazedly if this instant physical connection was what romantics meant when they talked about love at first sight, or if the overwhelming affinity she felt was only her hormones reacting to his male chemistry.

Quinn saw the heat that flushed her fair skin and the sensual lethargy that lowered thick lashes over her drowsy blue eyes. Her body was delicate and infinitely feminine in his arms. A swift surge of unfamiliar emotion rocked him as a sudden flash of insight told him she fit against him as if her curves had been carved purposely to accommodate the harder angles of his own body.

"That didn't sound like no," he murmured, his voice husky with restraint.

"No, it didn't, did it?" she whispered.

Quinn didn't ask again. The need to feel her mouth under his was overwhelming. He tilted his head and his lips found the soft, outer corner of hers. She gasped softly, one swift indrawn breath that parted her lips, and he brushed his mouth along the lower curve of hers, tracing its velvety softness and beyond to the opposite corner before he carefully settled his mouth over hers, slowly fitting them seamlessly together.

Shielded from the other dancers by Quinn's broad shoulders, Victoria was adrift in a world bounded by Quinn's arms and the magic of his warm mouth wooing hers.

The sudden cessation of the music and the bandleader's voice announcing a break was a rude intrusion.

Quinn reluctantly lifted his mouth from hers, his brain foggy with desire. "The music stopped."

Victoria's senses were on overload. She'd never before been so aware of the differences between male and female. His arms wrapped around her, gently crushing the softer curved lines of her body against the harder planes of his. Distracted by the press of his body and the pleasantly abrasive brush of worn denim where his long legs aligned with her own bare limbs below the hem of her skirt, it took a long moment before she registered his words.

"Oh." She glanced over his shoulder. The dance floor was slowly emptying, couples retreating to booths and tables.

Quinn reluctantly released her waist, catching her hand in his. "I'll take you back to your table. Are you here with somebody?"

"Just my cousin." Victoria pointed across the room before smoothing a hand self-consciously over her hair. Her fingers twined in his, she started across the room.

The booth that had held only Nikki and Victoria when Quinn first saw her was crowded now. Quinn nodded to Doug Akers, SueAnne Gibbs, Nikki and Lonna Denning.

"There you are, Victoria," Lonna said. "I'm sorry that it took so long to get our drinks, but I was delayed by a friend who insisted that I dance with him."

"That's all right," Victoria replied. "I was dancing myself." She looked up at Quinn. He looked back, his green gaze going molten, and for a moment, she forgot that anyone else was present.

"Jeez, Quinn," Nikki blurted, her eyes round with surprise. "What are you doing with her—she's an attorney!"

Victoria laughed at the redhead's blunt shock, expecting Quinn to share her amusement.

But Quinn wasn't laughing.

He tensed, his big body going completely still. His eyes reflected shock and then an instant, blazing anger before they turned cool and unreadable. His hand released hers and although he only took a small step back, Victoria felt his distancing as if he'd thrown up a wall between them.

He nodded his head briefly at the quartet seated at the table.

"Goodnight, ladies—Doug." He glanced briefly at Victoria, his gaze polite and distant. "Thanks for the dance, Victoria."

Victoria was speechless. She watched him shoulder his way through the crowd until he disappeared through the arched doorway before turning to Lonna.

"What was that all about?" she demanded, stunned hurt and confusion quickly being replaced by growing anger at Quinn's abrupt departure.

The four occupants of the booth exchanged uncomfortable glances and shifted uneasily against the red vinyl seat. An unspoken message passed from Nikki to SueAnne.

"C'mon, Doug," SueAnne caught the cowboy's hand and tugged him after her out of the booth. "Dance with me—you don't want to hear this girl-talk."

"Thanks, SueAnne," Nikki said gratefully. "Sit down, Victoria."

Victoria glanced over her shoulder at the doorway where Quinn had disappeared before she allowed Lonna to tug her down onto the bench seat.

"So—" Victoria lifted a questioning eyebrow at Lonna. Her cousin's gaze met hers for a brief moment before she looked at Nikki. Victoria's glance followed Lonna's and found the redhead staring at her guiltily, her deep brown eyes worried and faintly embarrassed beneath the fine arch of her dark brows.

"I'm sorry, Victoria," Nikki said earnestly. "Me and my big mouth—I shouldn't have told him you're an attorney. I was so surprised to see him with you that I didn't think..." Nikki's shoulders lifted in a helpless shrug, and she turned to Lonna with a silent plea for help.

"Why would he care if I'm an attorney?" Victoria felt as if she'd started reading a mystery in the middle of the book.

"You're female and a lawyer," Lonna interjected. "And that means that you, Victoria Denning, are a leading candidate for Quinn's least favorite person."

"He doesn't like women lawyers? Why?"

"Because his stepmother hired a hotshot woman attorney from Helena to contest the will when his father died," Nikki said. "Local gossip claims that when Charlie Bowdrie passed away two years ago, he left the bulk of his estate to Quinn and Cully. His sons got most of the financial assets, including the machinery and livestock. Eileen got the house in town and a comfortable trust fund, but she was furious that the boys received more. So she took them to court. The case finally went to trial three months ago and the judge made a decision last week. I'm not sure what happened, exactly, but both Quinn and Cully hate Eileen Bowdrie's attorney. Gossip says she behaved like a real barracuda, raking up the illegitimacy of the boys, the scrapes they got into when they were kids...all sorts of things that didn't seem to have a lot of direct connection to the case. Cully said that Quinn was more furious with the attorney than with his stepmother. And of course," she added, "Quinn doesn't have a lot to do with women in general."

"He doesn't?" Victoria was dumbfounded. The man that made her bones melt when he smiled didn't like women? And when he'd kissed her... She shivered and pulled her wayward concentration back to Lonna and Nikki. "A bad experience like that might have soured him on women attorneys, but that doesn't explain why he doesn't like women in general.''

Lonna sighed. ''Unfortunately, his stepmother is probably the reason for that, too.'' She paused a moment before continuing. ''I don't like to repeat gossip, Victoria, but Eileen Bowdrie is a mean, spiteful woman. She and Charlie Bowdrie never had children—I don't know if they simply couldn't, or she wouldn't, but Charlie wanted sons. He had a liaison with a young woman in the next county that scandalized Colson and fathered two sons. No one knows what happened, but one day Charlie brought Quinn and Cully home with him and told Eileen that he was going to raise them on the ranch, whether she liked it or not. She's resented Quinn and Cully ever since, and rumor says she made their lives hell when they were growing up.''

''How old were the boys when they went to live with their father?''

''I think Quinn was about eight, which would make Cully four or five.''

Appalled, Victoria shook her head. ''That's terrible—they were so young. What happened to their mother?''

''No one knows. My mother told me that she simply disappeared. No one's seen her in all the years since.'' Lonna spread her hands in a gesture of helplessness. "Quinn keeps to himself and rarely dates. I don't know that it's accurate to say that he doesn't like women. I think it's more that he's very cautious and keeps a lot of distance between him and any interested women. As a matter of fact, I haven't heard of him taking a woman out since he was in high school." She lifted an eyebrow. "Although it's no secret that he's visited several willing women in neighboring counties over the years, I've never heard of him actually dating anyone." She glanced at Nikki for confirmation. "Have you?"

"No, never. He's always polite to me," she added. "But he's quiet. I certainly don't know him as well as I know Cully—and I can't claim to be really close to Cully." She smiled wryly. "Much as I wish I were. The truth is, there's something a little dangerous about the Bowdrie boys."

A small shiver of awareness raced up Victoria's spine.

"Dangerous?" she asked carefully. "What do you mean, exactly?"

"It's hard to explain." Nikki paused, a small frown creasing her brow. "Not only is there just something you feel when you're around them, but there's always some story circulating about them."

"She's right," Lonna agreed. "Though I'm skeptical about most of the stories. The last one I heard was a year or so ago when rumors said Quinn got a local girl pregnant and then paid her to leave town."

Victoria recoiled inwardly. "Was it true?"

"I doubt it."

"I don't believe a word of it." Nikki firmly echoed Lonna. "Cully and Quinn have always refused to deny rumors. They hate gossip. But if either of them knew that they'd fathered a child, they would have insisted on marrying the woman and raising the baby."

"The only part of the story that's confirmed is that Angie Patterson left town. The rest is pure speculation," Lonna added. "Personally, I think Quinn is a far better man than either he or his stepmother think he is. He and Cully grew up knowing they were illegitimate and so did everyone else in Colson. That set them apart. It's tough to be different in a town as small as Colson. Of course," she added with a twinkle, "it didn't help their reputations that they were both pretty wild when they were teenagers."

"That's true," Nikki agreed. "My favorite story is the one about Cully climbing the water tower and spraypainting it with red, white and blue stripes on the Fourth of July."

Victoria had a quick mental image of the town's medium-size water tower. ''The whole thing?''

''Almost. The mayor caught him before he finished. But the mayor was afraid of heights and wouldn't climb the ladder, so Cully ignored him and just kept painting until the sheriff arrived and went up to get him. I think he was about twelve at the time, and his dad had to bail him out of jail.''

Lonna laughed. ''I'll never forget the time they drove a herd of cattle through the middle of town. The merchants were furious, but Quinn told them his dad told him to move old man Johnson's cattle from his pasture outside town to the rodeo grounds on the other side of Colson. The shortest route was down Main Street. Since it was the merchants who'd asked Johnson to move the cattle, they couldn't convince the sheriff to charge Quinn and Cully with anything.

''And then there was the time Quinn broke his arm at the rodeo in the afternoon and that night, he rode again and won the bronc-riding competition.''

''With a broken arm?'' Victoria asked in disbelief.

''Yes—I suspect he'd numbed the pain with whiskey, but nonetheless, it must have hurt.''

"No wonder the Bowdries have reputations for being wild," Victoria commented dryly. "They *are* wild."

"No question that they certainly were when they were teenagers," Lonna agreed. "They dated the girls with the worst reputations and were the first boys questioned when anything crazy happened. But after their mid-twenties, they settled down."

"That's true," Nikki confirmed. "But they're still considered dangerous. Any woman who goes out with one of them is automatically on the top of everyone's gossip list." She shifted her red hair back over her shoulder, tucking it behind her ear with an absentminded gesture. "In spite of the rumors and gossip, though, the Bowdrie brothers are still the most eligible bachelors in the county—and the least likely to wed."

"I don't imagine that's surprising, given their background." Victoria frowned at the bottle of beer Lonna handed her. Her own life as a well-loved daughter had been quiet and safe. She'd been an intense, focused child who'd known from the time she was eight years old that she would become an attorney. Boys and dating hadn't been an important issue, and she'd never known anyone quite like Quinn Bowdrie. She wasn't sure what she wanted from Quinn, but to have him reject her before she had a chance to decide, and for reasons that had nothing to do with her personally, was frustrating. "So much for cowboys—I should have known better," she raised the bottle, swallowed with an unladylike gulp and choked. "Yuk! What is this stuff?"

Lonna laughed, her eyes twinkling at the look of disgust on Victoria's face. "Beer—would you rather have wine?"

"No," Victoria said with grim resolve. "I'm stuck in Montana for the next year—I'll learn to drink beer. Straight from the bottle." She closed her eyes, took another sip, and shuddered.

"I think it may take awhile." Nikki said dryly.

Lonna nodded. "I think you're right."

Chapter Two

Over the next two weeks, Victoria threw herself into a frenzy of activity transforming the apartment she had rented in the old Victorian house next door to Nikki's home into a welcoming nest. In the end, she was well satisfied with her home.

The activity focused her, gave her a purpose to fill her days and kept her too busy to fret over her problems. Her life as a child, teen and a young adult had been goal-oriented. She'd known from the day her uncle John had taken her and Lonna to the courthouse to watch his friend Hank Foslund plead a case that she would be a lawyer when she grew up. During her childhood, Victoria's father had driven his family from Seattle to his brother's home in Colson to spend their three-week summer vacation. She and Lonna were as close as sisters, and Victoria's parents often gave in to the girls' pleas to allow Victoria to spend an extra month with her cousin after they returned to Seattle. Many warm evenings had found the cousins challenging the widowed attorney to checker marathons on the screened porch. Those long summer evenings had cemented their friendship and her own resolve to practice law.

Now her health and her doctor's edict had taken away her career. Granted, it was a temporary situation, but still she felt cut adrift, anchorless and without purpose.

Victoria didn't like it, and she was determined to get her life back on track. The hiatus from her work was frustrating. So she threw herself into working on the apartment, clerking at her uncle John's pharmacy and filling in for Hank. Business at the law office was slow, for all of his clients knew that Hank had left on a much-needed vacation. Fortunately for Victoria, however, Hank's files were a disaster. She discovered that there was apparently no rhyme nor reason to his filing system, in fact, she couldn't decipher any system at all. Satisfied that here was a project that would

test even her fierce need for involvement, she
dived into the years of files and documents that
filled the cabinets in Hank's office.

Busy though she was, however, she found
thoughts of Quinn Bowdrie intruding all too often.
Irritated to find herself remembering the handsome rancher and the kiss they'd shared, she determinedly pushed the memory aside. Still, she
found she couldn't banish him from her dreams.

Just after lunch one afternoon, Victoria bent
from the waist and ran a feather duster over a
bottom shelf in the cosmetics section. Dennings
Pharmacy was enjoying a pleasant lull after a
busy morning. The early afternoon sun poured
through the plate-glass windows at the front of
the store, glittering off the decorative glassware,
bottles, and colored jars displayed in the deep
window embrasures. Victoria had already dusted
and efficiently reorganized the display before
moving on to the aisle counters.

Humming along with the country music playing
softly on the radio, she brushed the feather duster
over a jewel-toned collection of bottles filled with
nail polish. The store was quiet except for the low
murmur of voices as a customer chatted with her
uncle John at the pharmacy counter in the back
of the store.

The jingle of bells that hung on the front door

interrupted the soft music and Victoria stood, glancing across the store at the entrance. The small drugstore boasted only six aisles, the displays and shelves low enough for her to see over the top and across the width and length of the store from front to back.

That's odd. I'm certain I heard someone come in.

Her tennis shoes made no sound on the waxed tile floor as she walked to the end of the aisle. She rounded the end display and stopped in midstride. Her pulse accelerated and irritation warred with attraction before distraction won.

Quinn Bowdrie was halfway down the aisle, talking to an adorable, wide-eyed toddler. He sat on his heels, one knee touching the floor, his forearm resting on the other bent knee. A grey Stetson was pushed back off his forehead, revealing thick black hair. A pair of sunglasses crowded a pocket of his blue chambray work shirt, and faded jeans, worn white at stress points, molded the heavy muscles of his thighs.

"I got a car," the little boy announced importantly, and he held out one chubby hand, palm up.

"So you do." Quinn took the miniature red metal car from the little hand and balanced it on his palm. "That's a pretty nice set of wheels. Do you know what kind it is?"

"Yup—it's a 'Far-ee.' "

Quinn turned the die-cast metal car over and read the imprint.

"You're absolutely right," he said. "Ferrari—that's what it says."

"Where?"

The little boy stepped closer, stumbling over Quinn's boot, and he moved quickly to steady the small body, his hand splayed across the child's back.

Unnoticed by either of the two males, Victoria watched a rare, gentle smile break across Quinn's hard face as he looked at the child.

"Careful, partner." His voice was a deep-throated murmur, his big hand gently patting the small back reassuringly before he gravely inspected the little boy's offering.

The child peered at the car in Quinn's hand, studying the imprinted letters. "Right there?" He asked, tracing the upraised letters. "That says 'Far-ee?' "

"Uh-huh. How did you know this car is a Ferrari?" Quinn asked him.

"My daddy told me." The little boy said, nodding emphatically. "It's my favorite car—see, it's red."

"Ah." Quinn nodded sagely. "I see."

This is the tough rancher who has no heart?

Victoria thought with amazement. Watching the big man with the small boy brought a lump to her throat. She stood motionless, silently observing the two dark-haired heads bent together over the miniature car until Quinn glanced up. His green eyes darkened, an unnamed emotion flitting briefly across his hard features before his expression turned unreadable.

He slipped an arm under the little boy's denim-clad bottom and stood in one smooth motion, the child seated safely on his arm.

He didn't say anything. Victoria considered turning her back and walking away from him but thought better of the impulse.

"Hello."

"Hello." Quinn knew the moment he looked up and saw Victoria that he'd been lying to himself. He hadn't been able to forget her, nor the kiss they'd shared on the shadowy dance floor, despite the fact that he'd never met an attorney he liked. And he downright detested pushy, aggressive female lawyers. He'd been moody, irritable and restless for the last two weeks. His gaze flicked down her body, noting the blue smock with Dennings Pharmacy embroidered over the upper swell of her left breast. "What are you doing here?"

"I work here." Victoria's memory of black

hair, green eyes, tanned skin and a muscled, broad body wasn't exaggerated. If anything, Quinn Bowdrie was even more blatantly male than she'd remembered. And judging by the irritation on his handsome face, the anger that had blazed in his eyes at the Crossroads Bar hadn't diminished.

"You're a salesclerk? Isn't that a big step down from practicing law?" Quinn shifted the little boy on his arm. Her voice was frostily reserved, and the soft smile that had dazed him while they danced was noticeably absent.

"Some people might say so. However, I'm also handling Hank Foslund's emergency calls and doing some other work for him for the next month or so. I happen to believe that work is work, regardless of the occupation. While I have a law degree and practicing law is my profession, it's not the sum total of my existence," she said pointedly, her gaze narrowing over the shift in his expression as he registered her words. His jaw firmed, his eyes narrowed. She could swear he grew taller as he stiffened. "My doctor ordered me to stay away from stress for at least six months. So—" she gestured at the store around her, wielding the colored collection of feathers "—I'm a clerk."

"Six months? Do you really believe that you

can keep from meddling in other people's lives for six months?''

"I don't meddle in people's lives.''

"You're an attorney,'' Quinn said flatly. "Meddling in people's lives is how you make your living.''

"You're entitled to your opinion.'' Victoria held on to her temper with an effort. "But a lot of people, myself included, wouldn't agree with you. In fact, Mr. Bowdrie, a lot of people, myself included, might argue that your opinion is suspect because you're clearly prejudiced against attorneys.''

"Damned straight,'' he shot back.

"Bobby? Where are you?'' The female voice interrupted Quinn.

"Uh-oh.'' The little boy in Quinn's arms patted his face, demanding his attention. "That's my mama.''

A young woman in her early twenties rounded the end of the aisle, her harassed expression quickly changing to relief and exasperation as she spied them.

"Bobby! There you are.'' She walked down the aisle toward them and held out her arms.

Quinn handed the little boy to his mother, and she settled him against her hip with practiced ease.

"He wasn't a bother."

The young mother's guarded gaze flicked from Quinn to Victoria before she smiled at her son. "I thought he was right behind me, playing with his car, while I talked to Mr. Denning. Then I turned around and he was gone." She smoothed a lock of black hair from the little boy's forehead.

"Thanks." Her quick glance included both Quinn and Victoria before she hurried away down the aisle, the bells on the front door ringing melodically as the pair disappeared outside.

Quinn turned back to Victoria.

"I'd better be going, too."

The cowboy who had smiled gently at the toddler was gone, replaced by a remote, hard-faced stranger. This Quinn was the man that had walked away from her at the Crossroads Bar and Grill after kissing her nearly senseless. She'd neither forgotten nor forgiven how easily he'd turned off the heat while she still felt singed. Besides, she was angry enough with Quinn's unreasonable prejudice against her occupation that the urge to needle him was irresistible.

"Aren't you forgetting something?"

A faint frown creased his brow. "Not that I know of."

Victoria gestured at his empty hands. "Didn't

you come in here to buy something, or were you just browsing?''

''No, I didn't stop to browse.'' He slipped his fingers into his shirt pocket and removed a folded paper. ''A neighbor asked me to drop off this prescription.''

She took the slip of paper and unfolded it, frowning slightly as she struggled to decipher the scribbled words.

Quinn took advantage of her distraction to study her unobserved. The blue pharmacy smock she wore was hip length; unbuttoned, it hung open from throat to hem. Beneath it, she wore a scoop-necked white T-shirt tucked neatly into belted khaki shorts that hit her at midthigh. Below the narrow hem of the shorts, her legs were long, curvy and lightly tanned. White socks with neatly folded down tops and tennis shoes covered her small feet. Her hair was a smooth fall of silvery silk that brushed her shoulders, only the bangs were faintly ruffled where she'd sifted her fingers through them as she talked. She reminded him of a well-cared-for, sleek little blue-eyed cat. And he wanted to cuddle her, stroke and pet her just to see if he could make her purr.

It irritated the hell out of him that he couldn't seem to stop wanting to touch her.

''...don't you think?''

Quinn realized that he'd missed the question, whatever it was.

"I, uh..."

Victoria glanced up from the prescription to find him staring at her. His gaze lingered on her breasts before stroking upward to focus intently on her mouth. Her heartbeat thudded faster, and she caught her breath, awareness flaring between them.

"If you weren't so prejudiced against lawyers," she murmured, "I'd ask you over for dinner."

Quinn went completely still. His eyes went hot, and he stared at her for a long moment.

"But I am, and even if I weren't, I don't think seeing you is a good idea." His deep voice was quiet, undertones of tension humming beneath the simple refusal.

"But..."

Too late. Even as Victoria started to protest and ask him to explain, he was gone. His long strides carried him swiftly down the aisle to the front of the store, the bells tinkling as he pulled the plate-glass door open and disappeared through it.

She stared at the empty doorway, regret mixed with irritation.

Men. Who can understand them? And cowboys seem to make less sense than general, run-of-the-mill guys. Maybe working outside in all that fresh air affects their brains!

She shook her head and returned to her dusting, determined not to spend another minute thinking about Quinn Bowdrie.

Unfortunately, Victoria discovered over the next week that commanding herself not to waste brain power thinking about the handsome rancher and actually accomplishing it were two very different things.

Saturday morning found her seated cross-legged on the floor of Hank Foslund's office, a pile of file folders on her lap. Behind her, the top drawer of a low filing cabinet stood open, the files that had crammed its now-empty space surrounding her in a circle of neatly labeled stacks. She'd been pulling and organizing files for two hours, finishing the *A*'s and moving on to the *B*'s.

She scanned the last three remaining folders and shifted them off her lap, placing them in the proper alphabetical stack.

"Hank," she muttered to herself with a fond shake of her head. "You may be a great attorney, but you're terrible at organization. You should have hired another file clerk when Shirley retired."

She pushed the top drawer closed and pulled

open the bottom one. Like its mate, it too was crowded full of files, loose papers jammed haphazardly to hang half-in, half-out of folders.

The first file was so thick that she had to slide both hands beneath it to lift it from the drawer. The sides bulged and when she set the folder on the floor, it popped open, papers slithering loose to slide across the carpet.

Exasperated, Victoria shuffled the papers together before settling cross-legged once again to attach loose pages and reorganize the file. One look at the heading on the topmost document, however, had her mouth dropping open.

She hadn't known that Hank Foslund represented the Bowdries.

But I should have, she realized. He's the only attorney in town, and he's represented most of the ranchers for years.

Feeling almost guilty, Victoria tried to deal with the file in an objective, professional manner. But she had to read at least a portion of each document in order to determine in which section of the big file the paper should be placed.

It became quickly obvious that the contents related to Eileen's attempt to break Charlie Bowdrie's will. It was also clear that Eileen had alleged that her husband had been mentally incompetent after suffering a stroke. Her attorney

had used the public forum to villify Quinn and
Cully, contending that Charlie was clearly not of
sound mind or he would not have left his valuable
property to two such unworthy recipients.

Victoria frowned and flipped through the pages
to the original document. Her frown deepened as
she read the allegations and double-checked the
date of the will against the date of Charlie's ill-
ness and subsequent death.

He made the will years before he suffered the
stroke that eventually killed him. She shook her
head, considering the significance of the dates.
The attorney representing Eileen Bowdrie must
have known there was little basis for filing this
lawsuit, she mused. No wonder Quinn dislikes attorneys. It seems clear that the only reason this
suit was filed was malice.

She shook her head in disgust and went back
to sorting and attaching documents into the thick
file until at last, there were only two sheets of
paper left. The two letters were from a law firm
in Helena, and both appeared to be an annual report on the status of a trust fund of some sort.
Although the name Bowdrie was scrawled across
the top of the letters in Hank's bold, almost illeg-
ible hand, the file number below the name wasn't
the same as the thick file spread open on the floor
before Victoria.

She paper-clipped the two letters together and added them to the stack of misfiled documents on top of the filing cabinet. Then she slipped the thick Bowdrie file back into its place in the file drawer. A quick glance at her watch told her she was going to be late for dinner with Aunt Sheila and Uncle John.

She quickly gathered her purse and let herself out of the office, carefully locking the door behind her, the puzzling letters forgotten on top of the cabinet.

Struggling to deal with the culture shock of her sudden shift from city to small town life, Victoria found herself brewing tea at two on Sunday morning, unable to sleep. She wasn't sure if her sleeplessness was due to the lack of traffic noise outside or the hazy dream she'd had about dancing with Quinn.

Whatever the cause, Victoria stifled a yawn and struggled to concentrate on the minister's sermon much later that morning.

Oh, what I'd give for a double shot latte, she thought longingly. Flavored coffee brewed strong enough to jolt her awake was only one of a long list of things she missed about Seattle. Six months, she lectured silently. I will make the best of living away from city comforts for the next six months.

Later, as she followed her aunt down the aisle and stepped out into the sunshine, she reminded herself that there were many things she enjoyed about living in this small Montana town. The pleasure of breathing air untainted by city exhaust, the friendliness of neighbors and the opportunity to spend time with her aunt, uncle and cousin were only a few of the reasons she liked Colson. *I need to focus on what I enjoy about living in Montana,* she thought. *And not on what I miss about Seattle.*

"Hello, Sheila."

A plump, middle-aged woman, flowers bobbing atop her white straw hat, halted Sheila Denning. Victoria's aunt paused on the wide sidewalk, Lonna and Victoria beside her.

"Good morning, Laura, everyone." Sheila smiled pleasantly at the two women standing in a semicircle with Laura Kennedy. "I don't think you've met my niece, Victoria. She's recently moved to Colson. Victoria, I'd like you to meet Laura Kennedy, Becky Sprackett and Eileen Bowdrie."

"Good morning, it's a pleasure to meet you," Victoria murmured in response to the chorus of greetings. The woman that Sheila had introduced as Eileen Bowdrie piqued her interest. The impeccably dressed older woman had elegant features, but her patrician beauty was marred by cold blue eyes and a haughty air.

"I've met your relative—Quinn Bowdrie."

Eileen Bowdrie's eyes grew icier and she stiffened.

"I am most certainly *not* related to Quinn Bowdrie. Nor to his brother, Cully," she said emphatically. "If you were more familiar with our town, you'd know that those two are absolutely *no* blood relation of mine. I'm their father's widow, but I am certainly *not* their mother. Unfortunately for the community, they inherited all of their father's weaknesses and none of his strengths. They ought to be locked up somewhere, there isn't a decent woman in the county that's safe with either of them."

Despite Lonna and Nikki's description of Eileen, Victoria was still stunned by the woman's bitter attack. Her shock quickly gave way to anger, however, as bitterness continued to pour out of the woman. Stubborn and impossible though Quinn had been, Victoria thought, he'd gone out of his way to step in when Sam Beckman had proven difficult. Even when he'd discovered that she was an attorney he'd been angry but polite.

At last the woman paused to catch a breath.

"An interesting viewpoint," Victoria interjected smoothly. "However, my experience with Quinn was quite different. In fact, if it hadn't been for Quinn Bowdrie, I would have had to fight off the unwanted attentions of a local rancher at the Crossroads several weeks ago. I'm very grateful that Quinn was there and stepped in, and I found him to be a perfect gentleman."

Eileen's face flushed with anger, and her thin body stiffened. She seemed to expand and grow taller with affront.

"Well! I refuse to stand here and waste my time being corrected by a young woman who clearly has no understanding of this situation." Eileen glared at Victoria before turning a fulminating stare on her aunt. "Sheila, I suggest you apprise your niece of the facts." She switched her furious gaze back to Victoria. "And after you are aware of the true situation, I shall expect a full apology from you, young woman."

Clutching her purse between a rigid elbow and the cream silk suit covering her thin waist, Eileen Bowdrie turned on her heel and stalked away down the sidewalk, nearly vibrating with self-righteous fury.

"Well, I…" Laura Kennedy managed a feeble smile. "I'll see you ladies at the Garden Club meeting on Tuesday." She hurried off after Eileen, the flowers on her hat dipping and swaying in time with her quick strides.

"Well," Sheila declared in a puff of sound, before she eyed her niece. "You stirred up a hornet's nest, Victoria."

Victoria was so angry she could feel her cheeks radiating heat. "That is the most obnoxious woman I have ever had the misfortune to meet." She paused to draw a deep breath, exhaling slowly in an attempt to rid herself of the anger that coursed through her veins and beat at her temples. "Outside of opponents in divorce court, I've never heard such vicious comments."

"Hah!" Becky Sprackett snorted inelegantly. "That wasn't as bad as some things I've heard her say." One capable, work-roughened hand patted Victoria's shoulder approvingly and she smiled, her faded blue eyes twinkling. "Good for you, girl. I'm glad you stood up to her. I think it's about time somebody reminded her that not all the folks in the county agree with her about the Bowdrie brothers."

"Becky's right," Sheila commented. "Eileen just isn't rational about those boys and never has been. To listen to her talk about them, a person would think that they had horns, tails and carried pitchforks."

"That's a perfect description of Eileen Bowdrie's ridiculous opinion," Becky declared with a sniff of disgust. "I've known those boys ever since they came to live next door at their daddy's ranch," she said firmly. "And they've never done anything worse than snitch a warm pie off my windowsill. Of course, they were a mite wild growing up. But their father, bless his soul, would be proud of the men they've become, despite what Eileen says."

"I've never met Cully, but I've met Quinn and saw no evidence of horns or a pitchfork," Victoria said.

"Hmm, that's right. You told Eileen that you met Quinn," Sheila murmured, eyeing her niece with interest. "And where was that, exactly?"

"At the Crossroads Bar and Grill—the night that Lonna and I went to hear a band she loves. And then I saw him again last Friday when he came into the pharmacy."

"He was in the pharmacy?"

"Yes. He dropped off a prescription—I believe it was yours, Becky."

Victoria noted the raised eyebrows and speculative glances between her aunt and Becky, but before she could question them, the minister joined their group and her query was forgotten in the ensuing conversation.

* * *

"Hey, Quinn!"

Cully's shout, followed by the slamming of the front door, shattered the silence of the ranch house.

"I'm in the kitchen," Quinn yelled. He glanced over his shoulder and watched his brother enter the room before he turned back to the sink. Dirty water ran from his soapy hands and swirled down the drain. Mud freckled his face, dotted his hair, splattered his shirt and coated his jeans almost to the knee. Only his feet, covered in white socks, were free of the half-wet, half-dry brown mud.

"What happened to you?" Cully asked, halting in midstride to stare.

"I got the truck stuck in that bog out in Pilgrim's Meadow."

"No kidding. What does the truck look like?"

Quinn glanced up and caught the amused grin that lit Cully's green eyes and tilted his mouth.

"Worse than I do." He said drily. He bent and ducked his head under the spigot, scrubbing his face and hair vigorously under the running water before he twisted the faucet closed. Eyes shut, he fumbled for the towel on the countertop and dried water from his face and hands before he turned back to Cully, his head buried in damp terry cloth as he rubbed his hair. "So," he mumbled, "where have you been?"

"Over at Becky's, helping fix her corral gate."

Quinn frowned and tossed the wet towel back onto the countertop. Cully's voice was filled with amusement. Quinn eyed him. His brother leaned against the counter, boot-covered feet crossed at the ankles, his arms folded across his chest. He was the very picture of innocence.

Quinn was instantly suspicious.

"At Becky's, huh?"

"Yup."

"Okay, I'll bite. What happened at Becky's that's so funny?"

"Becky went to church this morning."

"What's funny about that? Becky goes to church every Sunday morning."

"Yeah, but this Sunday morning the druggist's niece was there, too."

Quinn stiffened. "So?"

"So was our wicked stepmother."

Quinn's hands curled into fists. "What did she do to Victoria?"

"It's not what Eileen did to Victoria, it's what Victoria did to the wicked stepmother."

"All right, get to the point—what happened?"

"Victoria must not have known that Eileen hates our guts because she asked her if she was related to us. Becky says Eileen practically exploded and the longer she ranted about us, the angrier the niece got. According to Becky, the lady interrupted her in midspeech and verbally ripped her to shreds.'' Cully chuckled. ''Becky told me that Eileen swelled up like a balloon, she was so mad. Then she told the niece that she was owed an apology and stomped off.''

''Hell.'' Quinn uncurled his fists and thrust his fingers through his hair. ''What did she do that for?''

''Damned if I know,'' Cully said bluntly. ''But it's nice to know that somebody besides Becky has the guts to tell Eileen to shut up every now and then.'' He eyed Quinn with curiosity. ''Why did she stick up for us, anyway? Becky says the niece knows you—when did you meet her?''

''A couple of weeks ago at the Crossroads,'' Quinn replied, distracted by the mental image of what Victoria might have looked like angry. The smooth skin of her cheeks would have been flushed, her blue eyes snapping, her small body defensive.

''At the Crossroads?'' Cully's eyebrows lifted in surprise. ''Is this the blonde Nikki told me you took away from Sam Beckman?''

''I didn't take her away from Beckman,'' Quinn said impatiently. ''He was giving her a hard time and I cut in to dance with her. That's all. End of story.''

"Yeah. Right." Cully's tone was patently disbelieving. "If that's the end of the story, then how come she jumped down Eileen's throat when she started complaining about you?"

"Who knows?" Quinn shrugged. "She's an attorney. Maybe it's just a natural reaction for her to argue."

"Hmm. Possibly, but I doubt it—sounds to me like the lady likes you, Quinn."

"I doubt it, but if she does, she'd be smarter to keep it to herself," Quinn said grimly. "If the gossips in Colson decide she's interested in a Bowdrie, her reputation will be toast."

Cully's face tightened, his eyes narrowing.

"Yeah," he agreed, his voice hard.

The kitchen was silent for several moments while the brothers were immersed in their own thoughts before Cully glanced at Quinn in slow surprise.

"She's an attorney? Did you say the Dennings's niece is an attorney?"

"Yeah."

Cully whistled, a soft, almost silent pursing of his lips.

"Well, I'll be damned. You not only spoke to her, you actually went out of your way to take her away from Beckman?"

"I told you—I didn't take her away from Beckman."

"But she's an attorney. You hate women attorneys. We both do."

"Yeah, well, I didn't know she was an attorney when I danced with her, okay?"

"Okay." Cully lifted his hands in surrender. He started toward the doorway to the back porch. "Must be some woman."

And with that parting shot, he walked across the small utility room and disappeared outside, the screen door slapping shut behind him.

Quinn glowered at the closed door. Cully's departing figure was clearly visible through the mesh screen and his cheerful whistling was plainly audible.

There was no question that Cully thought he'd discovered a chink in Quinn's armor and would continue to tease him about Victoria.

"Damn," Quinn swore as he threw his mud-splattered shirt inside the washer before stripping off his jeans and heading upstairs for a shower.

Moments later, he stood under the pounding stream, sluicing the remaining mud from his hair. He braced his hands against the tiled wall and let the hot spray knead his sore back muscles.

Why was she defending him? He'd given her no cause.

The question nagged Quinn the rest of the day and into the evening. He wanted to ask her why she'd championed him in front of her aunt and her friends but he knew he shouldn't. He should stay away from her.

Victoria was curled up in bed, reading, when someone knocked on her apartment door.

She glanced at the alarm clock on her nightstand. "Ten o'clock?" She couldn't think of anyone who might be visiting her except Lonna, and she'd already spoken with her cousin earlier in the evening. Nevertheless, she grabbed her comfortable cotton wrap robe from the foot of her bed and headed into the living room. The old-fashioned oak door was heavy and solid, with no peephole marking its thick panels. She paused, her hand hesitating on the doorknob, made cautious by her years in Seattle and the lateness of the hour.

"Who's there?"

"Quinn Bowdrie."

Startled, Victoria stared at the oak panel for a moment before she twisted the dead bolt free and pulled open the door.

"Hello."

"Hi."

Quinn stared at her silently. Nonplussed, Victoria could only stare back. What was he doing here?

He glanced over her shoulder at the lamplit room beyond. He tilted his head to look down at her and the brim of his Stetson threw a faint shadow over the top half of his face.

"Can I come in?"

"Yes, of course."

She stepped back hastily and waved him into the room. He moved past her and she closed the door, leaning against it for a moment while she stared at the blue chambray covering his broad back and shoulders. Her gaze swept down the long length of his legs encased in faded jeans and vaguely noted the black cowboy boots he wore while she struggled to get her bearings. What was he doing here? After he'd flatly rejected the possibility of visiting her at the pharmacy, he was the last person she'd expected to see at her door.

Quinn glanced around the room before he turned to face her.

"I'm surprised to see you." She pushed away from the door, tugged the robe sash tighter and eyed him. "Didn't you tell me that visiting me wasn't a good idea?"

"I did." He nodded briefly. "And I still don't think it's a good idea."

Victoria's eyes narrowed. "Then what are you doing here?"

"I heard you had a run-in with my stepmother this morning. I wanted to thank you for defending me..."

Victoria's militant stance softened, a half smile curving her lips.

"...and tell you not to do it again."

The smile disappeared and she frowned.

"That's a left-handed thank-you if I ever heard one, and I've heard some pretty grudging thank-yous."

Quinn yanked his Stetson off and raked the fingers of his right hand through his hair. "I didn't mean to sound ungrateful. I appreciate your standing up to my stepmother, but you're wasting your time. Nothing you or anyone else can say will change what she thinks about my brother and me. All you're going to do is stir up the gossips and start them speculating about your own character. Before you know it, the stories making the rounds will be wilder than you can imagine. I don't want your good name ruined because of me—this isn't Seattle. Small town gossip can be brutal."

"Why do you care? I thought you believed that the fact that I'm an attorney automatically gave me a bad name."

"That's your profession—and your choice. This is personal and involves me."

"It was just one small conversation with a few women." Victoria waved her hand impatiently. "You're overreacting, Quinn. And even if you're right about this, I refuse to worry about small-minded people."

"You'd better worry," Quinn said grimly. "They can make your life hell."

Victoria shrugged. "I won't be here forever—six months isn't that long. And when I go back to Seattle, they'll forget about me and find someone else to talk about. In the meantime, I won't listen to your stepmother spreading wild lies about you."

"What makes you so sure that she's lying?"

"Oh, for heaven's sake," Victoria said impatiently. "Don't tell me that you expect me to believe that nonsense she told me."

Her unquestioning belief in him was astounding. With the exception of Becky, Quinn couldn't remember anyone else ever telling him that Eileen was dead wrong about him. A swift stab of emotion pierced his chest and he absentmindedly rubbed his fingers over his heart in an attempt to erase the pain.

Victoria's gaze flicked to his fingers and then back to search his face.

"What's wrong?"

Concern edged her tone.

Quinn quickly dropped his hand away from his shirt.

"Nothing." He had to get out of her apartment and away from her. The quiet room, lit only by the soft glow of a lamp, was too intimate. He'd tried, and failed, to ignore the robe that clung to her curves and left her legs bare from just above her knees to her toes. Now he tamped down the urge to smooth his palm over her normally sleek blond hair that was tousled as if she'd just gotten out of bed. But the spark of worry and caring in her eyes was an enticement he could barely resist.

I have to get out of here. Now.

He settled his hat on his head and moved forward.

"Take my advice," he said brusquely. "Stay away from Eileen. And don't defend me. Don't even admit you know me."

"No." Victoria's chin firmed stubbornly and she crossed her arms across her chest.

Don't do that. Quinn almost groaned. The move pulled her robe taut across her chest, deepening the V opening to reveal the beginning slope of her breasts and an edge of green silk. His palms itched and he curled his fingers in over them.

"I refuse to agree to something that I know is wrong."

She didn't budge from her position in front of the door. Quinn took a step nearer, but still she didn't move.

"You don't have to agree, just don't defend me again." He glanced at the door behind her. "It's not a good idea to have my truck parked outside your apartment building for long. I have to leave."

Exasperated, Victoria didn't budge. "You have an annoying habit of ending conversations by walking away from me."

"And you have a habit of not listening."

He closed his hands over the slope of her shoulders, intending to shift her aside, but the feel of warm woman beneath thin cloth distracted him. He smoothed his thumbs over the smooth cotton, tracing the delicate line of her collarbone. Her eyes darkened and she caught her breath.

"This isn't a good idea," he muttered, fighting the need to pull her into his arms.

Chapter Three

Victoria wanted him to kiss her. She recognized the unmistakable signs that Quinn wanted her, too. The hard line of his mouth was unrelentingly sensual, his nostrils flared as he drew a deep breath, his eyes a heated green between lowered lids. Her knees weakened, the floor beneath her feet shifted. She reached for the solid bulk that was Quinn, steadying herself with her palms against his chest.

"Why isn't this a good idea?" she asked, her voice a husky murmur in the hushed, expectant silence of the room.

"Because you're a safe, settled woman. And I'm not the boy-next-door."

"What makes you think I want the boy-next-door? Maybe I like dangerous men."

The grip of callused fingers tightened reflexively, his thumb stroked across soft cotton and found silky skin. His gaze flicked to her mouth and downward to her throat.

"Not a good idea." He murmured, distracted by the contrast of his work-roughened fingers, dark against her pale throat. He smoothed his palm upward over satiny skin, his fingers closing gently over her nape beneath her hair, his thumb stroking up the vulnerable arch of her throat. "A woman is likely to lose her good reputation—and a lot more."

His voice was a husky growl, taut with restrained hunger. Victoria's heart leapt wildly at the promise implicit in his words. Her pulse raced, hammering against the pad of Quinn's thumb where it rested in the hollow of her throat. He froze, muscles tensing, and his gaze lifted to meet hers.

Mesmerized, Victoria could only stare helplessly at the heat that blazed from his green eyes. She saw reluctance give way to acceptance, saw his lashes lower as he moved closer, bending slowly until his mouth touched hers.

Then her own lashes lowered, her hands fisting tightly in his shirtfront. For a long moment his mouth, carefully restrained, tasted hers. But the heat grew steadily stronger, hotter, and Victoria pressed closer, slipping her arms around his neck.

Quinn groaned against her mouth and slipped his arm around her waist. One big hand cradling her head, he eased her back against the door and half lifted her to fit her much smaller body more intimately against his bigger frame. She responded with an instinctive wiggle of hips to adjust to him and Quinn felt the leash on his control slip dangerously.

I have to stop. Warning bells clanged, disaster whistles blew.

Victoria stroked his bottom lip with her tongue.

Damn. I have to stop this. Now. His whole body clenched in refusal.

He broke the seal of their mouths with slow reluctance. Her lips clung to his and when he opened his eyes, the dazed passion in hers and the faintly swollen, damp curve of her lips almost sent him over the edge.

"We have to stop," he rasped.

"Why?"

She sounded as confused and aroused as he felt.

"Because we either stop now, or I pick you up and carry you to bed and finish this."

She stared at him, uncomprehending, until the words registered and recognition replaced passion.

"Oh."

"Yeah. Oh." Quinn mourned the loss of the soft weight of her breasts as he stepped back. She swayed and he caught her, tucking her against him once more for an all too brief moment before she pushed away from him. He shifted her aside and pulled open the door. "This won't work, Victoria. I won't be back. Find yourself a nice, safe man—and forget this happened."

Victoria didn't answer. With one last look, he stepped outside. The door closed with a quietly decisive click and she heard the sound of his boots as he took the stairs with long strides. She crossed the room, watching from the window as he walked down the sidewalk, started his truck and drove away.

He's impossible. Victoria stared at the dark, silent street outside. *What am I going to do about him?* She dropped the curtain and crossed to the door.

What led a man to tell a woman that he disliked her because of her occupation only to follow the statement by kissing her senseless? Why would a man who admitted that he deserved his bad reputation go out of his way to warn her and protect her from gossips? She'd dated men whose only interest in her was notching another sexual conquest on their bedpost. None of them had warned her nor worried about her good name and she doubted the possibility had ever crossed their shallow minds.

His gallantry with her and the gentleness she'd observed when he'd spoken to the toddler were at odds with his stepmother's bitter description of his character. And contradicted his own warnings.

Quinn Bowdrie was an enigma, she decided, twisting the dead bolt lock on the door. *The only thing about Quinn that I'm sure of,* she thought as she reentered her bedroom and climbed into bed, *is that he makes my toes curl when he kisses me and that he's fascinating.*

She wanted to get to know him better, wanted to learn if her instinctive belief that depth, humor and kindness lay beneath Quinn's hard exterior were true or not. But first she would have to convince him to spend time with her, and he seemed hell-bent on avoiding her.

I have six months in Colson. Six months to change his mind, get to know him and have some fun. After all, she rationalized, *we're both adults.*

Satisfied that she'd resolved the issue with her usual approach of clear logic and reasoning, she punched her pillow and turned off the light. She was a woman who needed goals and projects. Since she couldn't work on her professional career for the next six months, she'd work on developing her skills with interpersonal relationships. Quinn Bowdrie was an intriguing project that would productively occupy her time over the next few months.

The following weekend, the parking lot of the Crossroads Bar and Grill was packed, cars and pickup trucks nearly rubbing fenders or bumpers. Saturday night business was booming.

Lonna eased her little car into a narrow space at the end of a row and Victoria slipped out of the car, idly surveying the surrounding area while she waited for her cousin to join her.

The Bar and Grill was a single-story, long cement block building that took up one of the four corners of a crossroads where the state highway bisected a wide, oiled county road on the outskirts of Colson. Directly across the highway was a gas station, its pumps and office dark, closed up tightly for the night.

A warm breeze moved across the dark prairie that surrounded Colson, carrying the scent of sage on air untainted by city exhaust. Victoria drew a deep breath and tilted her face to the night sky. The gentle wind lifted her hair, sending silky strands skimming across her face. She brushed them back over her shoulder just as Lonna joined her.

"You're going to like the band that's playing tonight." Lonna linked arms with Victoria and set off toward the low building.

The pounding beat of bass and drums reverberated through the concrete block walls of the Bar, growing more distinct as they neared.

Victoria lifted an eyebrow in patent disbelief. "Really?"

"Really. Trust me, they're great."

"Well, they're certainly loud," Victoria conceded.

Lonna laughed and pulled open the heavy door to the wide entry hall. Victoria drew one last deep breath of the fragrant prairie air and followed her cousin inside.

The thick door opened into a foyer and a wave of music, noise, and cigarette-smoke-laden air greeted them. Blue neon spelled out *Grill* over the archway to their right, and Lonna walked beyond to the second archway where red neon proclaimed *Bar*.

She halted in the doorway beneath the neon sign and Victoria peered over her shoulder into the long, low-ceilinged room. The Bar was even more crowded than the last time they were here.

She wondered if Quinn was among the crowd, and her gaze searched the room.

"He's at the bar." Lonna leaned close to speak into Victoria's ear.

Victoria turned to look at her, and Lonna smiled with understanding.

"Quinn's standing at the end of the bar."

Victoria's gaze shifted, flicking over the row of men and women lining the long bar, stopping dead when she found Quinn at the far end.

"I see Nikki in a booth over there," Lonna shouted to make herself heard over the noise. "Let's join her."

A half hour later, Cully nudged Quinn.

"What?"

"Isn't that your blonde?"

Quinn stiffened and glanced over his shoulder to follow Cully's gaze. He located Victoria across the crowded dance floor, her hair gleaming silver beneath the lights as her partner swung her out and then back into his arms.

A stab of pure dislike for the man she danced with sliced into his chest and he turned back to the bar.

"Well?" Cully asked. "Isn't that her?"

"Yeah," Quinn growled. He drained the glass of beer that he'd been nursing for the last hour and gestured to the bartender for another. "That's her."

"Hmm. Not bad." Cully narrowed his eyes, assessing the couple. "No wonder you took her away from Beckman."

Quinn muttered under his breath. He didn't bother contradicting Cully.

"A woman who looks like that is wasted on Beckman," Cully continued.

Quinn glared pointedly at his brother. Cully grinned unrepentantly and returned to his conversation with a friend on his left.

Quinn stayed where he was when Cully and his friend left to circle the room. For a while, he nursed his beer and watched Victoria in the mirror behind the bar. She barely had time to slide into the booth where her cousin and Nikki sat before another man would claim her to dance.

He lost sight of her in the swirling crowd of dancers and turned, one elbow propped on the bar beside him, and searched the throng until he found her again. She was smiling at her partner, obviously enjoying herself.

Quinn seethed with fierce anger. He knew he had no right to feel betrayal, but that didn't change the way he felt. He'd never been jealous over a woman in his life, but there was no mistaking the nearly killing rage he felt each time another unsuspecting man slipped his arm around Victoria's waist to dance with her.

Across the room, Cully watched his brother watching Victoria. The colder Quinn's expression got, the more Cully's curiosity grew.

He left the table of men discussing cattle prices and ambled through the crowd to the booth where the pretty blonde sat with Nikki and Lonna.

"Hello, ladies."

"Cully!" Nikki's face lit with pleasure. She caught his arm and tugged him down onto the seat beside her. "When did you get here?"

"An hour or so ago," he responded, flashing her a smile before nodding a hello to the two women across the table. "How are you, Lonna?"

"Great, how about you?"

"Fine, just fine." His gaze switched to Victoria. "We haven't met, but I'll bet this is your cousin."

Lonna laughed and introduced Victoria. Curious, Victoria studied Quinn's brother. There was a strong family resemblance. Like Quinn, Cully's hair was raven-black, his eyes a slightly lighter shade of emerald beneath the arch of black brows. His face was just as strong-boned but more classically handsome than Quinn's. The same breadth of shoulder and powerful muscles marked his body although there was a slight edge about him while Quinn exuded a more controlled air of power. As strong as the resemblance was, however, Victoria felt none of the instant chemistry and connection to her heart that Quinn had generated.

"Rumor has it that you defended my brother against our stepmother," Cully commented.

"Sort of," Victoria said.

Lonna laughed. "Sort of? I don't think Eileen has had anyone cut off one of her tirades quite so neatly in her life. You should have been there, Cully, Victoria was wonderful."

"Yeah?"

"Lonna's exaggerating," Victoria protested, waving off the growing interest in Cully's expression. "I didn't do anything unusual, believe me."

"If you managed to make my stepmother speechless, then you definitely did something unusual," Cully said dryly. "That woman can go on for hours—and never say anything good."

"Then it's true that she makes a habit of attacking Quinn?" Victoria asked.

Cully eyed Victoria assessingly. He glanced at Nikki and Lonna, both listening with interest. "Quinn and I have a history with Eileen," he said without inflection. He stood. "Dance with me, and I'll tell you about it."

"All right." Victoria placed her fingers on his outstretched palm and slid out of the booth. He ushered her ahead of him to the less crowded end of the dance floor before taking her into his arms.

"You were going to tell me about your stepmother and Quinn," she prompted.

He grinned, his teeth flashing whitely against tanned skin. "That's right. But I'd rather you talked to me about you and Quinn. What's going on with you two?"

"I don't know what you mean." Victoria didn't hesitate, meeting his shrewd stare with blank innocence.

"I mean that my brother has been nearly impossible to live with for the past few weeks. Maybe it's a coincidence that his bad mood started the same day he met you, but I don't think so."

"Bad mood? Are you saying that I did something to upset your brother?" Victoria didn't know whether to be angry or hurt. She didn't like either option.

"Did you do something to upset him?" Cully grinned at her and lifted an eyebrow. "Oh, I think the fact that you're female and he's male was enough to do it."

Victoria's heart rate settled. "What exactly are you saying?" she asked bluntly.

"I'm saying that you've got my big brother running around in circles talking to himself. What I want to know is, what happened? Why are you dancing with every other guy in the place while he looks like he's contemplating murder across the room."

Startled, Victoria twisted in his arms to look over her shoulder at the long bar, but Quinn wasn't where she'd last seen him. It took a few moments to locate him where he leaned against the wall, alone at the far end of the dance floor. His grim expression left no doubt that he wasn't in a happy mood.

"He's contemplating murder?" she repeated, her gaze returning to Cully's.

"Close enough."

"Is that a good thing or a bad thing?" Victoria was beginning to hope that maybe Quinn was as dissatisfied with his "no contact" edict as she was.

"Hmm." Cully eyed her judiciously. "It's probably a bad thing for whoever's dancing with you if Quinn loses his temper. Fortunately, he rarely does. It might be a good thing if you happen to be looking for some proof that he's interested."

"Mmm." Victoria murmured.

Cully bent closer to search her face. "Can I take that to mean that you're interested?"

"Maybe," she responded noncommittally.

He narrowed his eyes in frustration.

"You're as bad as Quinn. Would it hurt you to tell me if there's a chance you'll put the poor guy out of his misery?"

"Cully..." Victoria began, then paused and stared at him, unsure.

"What?" he prompted.

She debated whether or not to be politely noncommittal. She decided in favor of bluntness. "Quinn's made it clear that he's not interested in spending time with me."

The disbelief on Cully's face told her that he didn't believe her.

"Quinn can be downright contrary, Victoria, but I've never known him to be stupid. And that would be stupid."

"Nevertheless," she said firmly, a shade of irritation seeping into her tone. "That's exactly what he said."

"Tell me what he said—exactly."

"He told me that he wouldn't be back—to find myself a safe man and to forget it happened."

"Forget what happened?"

The swift mental image of Quinn's mouth and body fused to hers sent color flooding up Victo-

ria's throat, heating her cheeks. "Never mind."
Cully's lips parted to form another question, and
she spoke quickly to forestall him. "I'm sure you
know your brother better than I do, but he certainly didn't seem confused about what he
wanted. And I haven't seen him since, so I have
no reason to believe that he's changed his mind.
So you see," she said firmly, "you must be
wrong. If your brother has been in a bad mood
lately, it isn't because of me."

"Hmm." Cully's gaze searched her features.
"And you're okay with this? You don't want to
see him, either?"

The quick emotion that swept Victoria was so
swift that she couldn't hide it. The instant, satisfied grin that curved Cully's lips told her that he
had his answer. Still, she shook her head.

"I'm not pining away because your brother
isn't interested in me, Cully," she said firmly.

"I can see that," he responded. He moved her
across the floor, deftly avoiding other couples as
he swung her out and back with quick steps.
"Both you and my brother are happy as can be—
couldn't be more pleased with the status quo,
right?"

"Right." Victoria had to concentrate on the
moves, ducking her head as he twirled her under
his arm.

"No hard feelings, just friends, right?"

"Right."

"Well, in that case, you won't mind dancing with him."

"Well, I don't know about..."

He ignored her protest. He swung her away from him and let go of her hand. Before Victoria could react, momentum sent her spinning into another body. Arms closed around her, hands gripping her waist. Even before she looked up, instinct told her who held her.

Quinn could have killed his brother, but the sheer relief of having Victoria in his arms made him decide to let Cully live. His gaze flicked over her startled face and then past her shoulder. His brother gave him a satisfied grin and turned his back to disappear into the crowd.

Shock gave way to awareness and Victoria tightened her grip on his forearms, her body tensing as she prepared to push away from him.

"Your brother..." she began, irritation seeping into her voice.

"Can be a real pain..." Quinn finished for her. His hands tightened at her waist, holding her against him. She looked up at him and frowned. "But every now and then, he does something right."

She stopped pushing against his arms, her body

resting lightly against his. "Is this one of those times?"

"Yeah," he said slowly, his gaze stroking over her flushed face. Her hair gleamed silver in the dim light and he lifted a hand to smooth it away from her cheek. Her skin was soft, warm beneath his fingertips and Quinn gave in to the need to hold her a little longer. "Dance with me."

It wasn't really a request, but Victoria nodded agreement nonetheless. He pushed away from the wall, shifting her backward, lifted her hands to his shoulders and wrapped his arms around her waist to tuck her against him.

Victoria closed her eyes and leaned into him, her forehead resting against the soft cotton shirt covering his shoulder. Warm, solid muscle shifted beneath her palms, fingers and forehead. The faintly rough cotton of his shirt brushed and caught on her silk blouse, teasing the tips of her breasts.

His arms tightened fractionally, urging her closer and she allowed it, seduced by the lure of warm male, drugged with the scent of the blend of faintly spicy aftershave, soap, fresh air and an indefinable unique scent that was Quinn.

"This isn't good," she murmured to herself.

"It's too good," Quinn's deep voice rumbled,

husky and strained, in her ear. "And that's a problem."

"You keep telling me that," she protested, opening her eyes and tipping her head back, just enough to meet his hooded gaze. "I'm having trouble accepting it."

"Maybe I've made a mistake." His eyes narrowed, his gaze intent. "Are you telling me that you're interested in an hour or two of great sex in the nearest motel?"

Victoria stiffened. "Is that all you're interested in? What about dinner and movies? There's more to a relationship between a man and a woman than great sex."

"Not for me," he said grimly. "I don't do relationships."

"Why not? If you ever tried getting to know a woman outside of a bedroom, maybe…"

"I've tried," he interrupted. "It didn't work."

"Why not?"

Quinn shrugged, his eyes bleak. "She told me that I was hot in bed and cold out of it."

"What does that mean?"

"It means, honey, that we could have great sex but I don't do relationships." His hand slipped lower, fingers splaying over her back just below her waist, and pressed her hips against his. "We'd burn up the sheets."

Victoria caught her breath. He was heavy, aroused, and as they swayed to the music, the slight movements of his hips against hers were powerfully seductive.

She fought to clear her passion-fogged brain.

"I want more than hot sex," she managed to get out, her voice unsteady.

His eyelids drooped lower, his eyes watchful as he searched her face.

"Most women do, honey."

"What makes you so sure all we could have is great sex?" she demanded, frustrated.

"Experience," he said flatly.

"Well, maybe you've just met the wrong women. Even dyed-in-the-wool rakes settle down sometime."

"Maybe. But it's not likely to happen with me."

He glanced over her shoulder. Although his arms still held her, Victoria could have wept at the distance that stretched between them.

The music stopped and he released her, taking a step back.

"Thanks for the dance."

"You're welcome," Victoria responded automatically, standing still, watching him walk away from her once again, threading his way through the crowd to disappear through the exit.

It wasn't until his broad back was no longer visible that Victoria glanced around and realized that he had left her a few steps from the booth.

She slipped onto the seat and lifted a longneck amber bottle, grimacing as the yeasty taste of beer hit the back of her throat.

"Well?"

She glanced up. Seated across from her, Lonna eyed her expectantly.

"Give, girl. You left with Cully and came back with Quinn. What happened?"

"Nothing."

Lonna huffed in disbelief. "Right. You're always this ruffled and flushed after a dance with any other guy in the room."

"Okay, you're right," Victoria conceded. "Quinn told me he doesn't do relationships. I gathered that's because he tried it once and it didn't work."

"Hmm. He must have been referring to that college thing."

"What college thing?"

"He was engaged while he was in college—senior year, I think. But I heard she broke it off."

Victoria's heart sank. "So he fell in love, his heart was broken and he's never gotten over her?"

"No, I don't think it was that. Gossip said he

was lucky since the ex-fiancée was mostly interested in money. It may have been true, since right after graduation, she married an older man who had fistfuls of cash and was willing to spend it on her. In any event, Quinn never acted like his heart was broken. Of course, with the Bowdries, it's hard to know exactly what they're feeling. It's not as if any of us are really close to either Quinn or Cully except maybe their neighbor, Becky Sprackett. They've always been a law unto themselves. My mother thinks it's because their father never hid their parentage, and Eileen was so horrible about it that the boys must have been affected.''

"It's difficult to imagine that they weren't," Victoria agreed, sympathy for the young boys vying with anger at the woman who had hurt them. "But that doesn't solve my problem," she continued, forcing her thoughts back to the present. "What am I going to do about Quinn?"

"Are you sure you want to do anything?" Lonna asked, eyeing her with concern. "I've never known you to react to a man like this, Victoria. Don't get me wrong," she added hastily. "I'm delighted that some guy finally distracted you from your single-minded obsession with your career. But Quinn is…well, he's Quinn. And you'll be going back to Seattle, and he'll be here in Montana. Are you sure you want to pursue this? It couldn't have been easy for Quinn when his fiancée broke their engagement. Do you want to chance becoming involved with him when you know you'll leave him too? Maybe Quinn is right, perhaps you should avoid each other while you're in Colson. You're not a one-night stand, 'affair' kind of person, are you?''

''No,'' Victoria sighed, turning the bottle in a slow circle on the tabletop. ''I'm not. And I have to confess that all the questions you just raised are ones that have occurred to me, too. But.'' She propped her elbow on the table, dropped her chin in her palm and her gaze met Lonna's. ''I've never met a man as...distracting...as Quinn. He makes me feel things I've only read about in books before. I know you and Nikki think Quinn might break my heart, but I've spent my whole life being careful. Quinn makes me want to take chances, be reckless. And isn't that what you told me I need?''

Lonna shook her head in disbelief. ''I never thought I'd see the day that my intelligent, practical, attorney cousin completely derailed. Honey, when I told you that you should learn to have fun and take chances, I was talking about working less, laughing more, dating some guys. I never meant for you to pick Quinn Bowdrie! That's like going from a bicycle to a nuclear rocket in one step."

"But you told me that you believe he's a better man than he thinks he is."

"I did—I do," Lonna said promptly. "But that doesn't mean that he won't break your heart."

"Nonsense." Victoria waved a hand dismissively. "That won't happen. I'll only be here a short time. Besides, I owe him a favor for fending off Sam Beckman for me."

"Hmm." Lonna couldn't hide her lack of conviction. "If you say so."

Victoria was no closer to resolving her mixed feelings about Quinn two days later when lunchtime arrived. She stripped off her pharmacy smock and walked next door to Annie's, a small cafe that served wonderful home-cooked meals.

The temperature had soared into the nineties, the hottest day since she'd arrived in Colson. She pushed open the plate-glass door and stepped into the cafe, sighing with relief as the air-conditioning dropped the temperature around her. Since the cafe was busy and there were no vacant stools at he counter, Victoria decided to bide her time and wait to be seated.

One of the women in front of her glanced over her shoulder. Victoria nearly groaned aloud as she recognized Eileen. Instead, she forced herself to nod a polite greeting.

"Good afternoon."

Mrs. Bowdrie sniffed and lifted her chin a notch higher. "Good afternoon." Her voice was frosty. Her eyes narrowed. "I understand that you ignored my warning."

"What warning was that?" Victoria said mildly, determined not to lose her temper with the difficult woman.

"About my stepsons." Her narrow body seemed to contract, her spine stiffening, her hands clutching her purse with a force that creased the expensive white leather. "You were seen dancing with not one, but both of them at a notorious bar."

A notorious bar? Victoria stared blankly at her for a moment before she realized what Eileen was referring to.

"My aunt and uncle have assured me that the Crossroads Bar and Grill is a completely respectable establishment," Victoria responded, hoping to distract the older woman from her obsession with Quinn and Cully.

"Hmph." Mrs. Bowdrie sniffed. "Just because most of the population of Colson can be found there on Saturday night doesn't make it respectable. And even if it were," she added, "that won't save your reputation after you were seen carrying on with Quinn Bowdrie.''

Victoria forced herself to count to five, slowly. "Just exactly what do you mean by carrying on, Mrs. Bowdrie?''

"Dancing and heaven knows what else in dark corners, Miss Denning.''

Victoria's teeth snapped together with a click. She could feel the flush of anger surge up her throat and heat her cheeks. Her patience disappeared. "Since when does dancing with a man in a public place qualify as carrying on?''

"Since you chose to do it with Quinn Bowdrie.''

Eileen's voice rose, carrying easily to the tables nearest the door. The occupants turned to stare, openly listening.

"I have a table for you, ma'am.'' The young waitress interrupted, nervously eyeing Victoria and Eileen. At that precise moment, the woman who had shared lunch with Eileen touched her arm tentatively.

"If we're going to make our one o'clock reading group, we should really leave, Eileen.''

"Very well.''

The woman smiled apologetically at Victoria and, chattering nonstop, eased Eileen out of the cafe.

Victoria, eyes narrowed angrily, frowned, unsure whether she was relieved or furious that the interruption had made it impossible for her to deliver a stinging reply.

"Ahem."

Victoria turned away from contemplating the door to find the waitress, menu in hand, waiting patiently.

"Oh. I'm sorry."

The girl's worried expression eased and she turned and led the way across the room to a table near a window. Still seething over Quinn's stepmother's remarks, Victoria seated herself and opened the menu while the waitress hurried away to fetch water. Victoria, her appetite gone, closed the menu with a snap, glancing up to discover that many of the cafe patrons were watching her. With an effort, she forced her facial muscles to relax and curved her lips in a smile, waggling her fingers in hello to a white-haired woman in a neat blue shirtwaist dress seated across the room. Becky Sprackett returned the wave and added a wink and a wide smile before she returned to her soup.

Fifteen minutes later, Victoria glanced up from her lunch salad to find Becky nearing her table.

"Hello," she said pleasantly, wondering what the blunt-spoken elderly woman wanted.

"Afternoon." Becky pulled out the chair opposite Victoria. "Mind if I join you?"

"No, not at all." Victoria waited as Becky settled her spare figure onto the wooden seat and set her handbag next to her. "How are you?" she asked politely.

"Arthritis has been acting up some, but other than that, pretty good. But I didn't sit down to talk about my health. I came over here to talk to you about Quinn."

Oh no. Victoria struggled not to sigh with exasperation and not to let her annoyance show on her face.

"I see," she said noncommittally.

"I doubt it." Becky eyed her assessingly. "Just what are your intentions toward that boy?" she demanded bluntly.

Chapter Four

"My..." Victoria got out. Speechless, she took a sip of water, choked, swallowed, carefully set the glass back on the blue-and-white checkered tablecloth and drew a deep breath before she squeaked. "My intentions?"

"That's what I said, girl." Becky pushed the water glass toward her. "Sounds like that went down your windpipe. Have another drink."

Wordlessly, Victoria obeyed.

Becky watched her down half the glass of water, listened as her coughing subsided and at last, nodded in satisfaction.

"There you go. Now, as I was saying, I'm the closest thing Quinn and Cully have to family. They barely knew their mama, their daddy's gone—rest his soul—and Eileen Bowdrie is worse than no stepmother at all. It's obvious to anybody with half a brain that Quinn's taken with you. Even Eileen has heard about it. The important question is, what do you think of him as a person."

Victoria had an instant mental image of Quinn on one knee, carefully steadying a little boy's stumbling, and decided to answer as bluntly as Becky had asked. "I think he's kind and caring, and I think he goes out of his way to convince people that he's just the opposite."

Becky visibly relaxed against the chair back.

"Good." She nodded approvingly. "If you know that about him, then you must be smart enough to figure out that Eileen's warnings are poppycock. He was a good boy, and he's a good man. I suspect that after listening to Eileen curse and rave all these years, Quinn—and Cully—have come to believe that she's right about them. But she's not." Becky fixed a stern gaze on Victoria and pointed an arthritis-gnarled forefinger at her. "And you may be just the one to convince Quinn they're all wrong."

"Me? Why me?"

"Hmph. In a town as small as Colson, a person

can't sneeze without everyone in town knowing that they have a cold. The gossips have been burning up the telephone wires ever since Quinn danced with you the first time at the Crossroads. The Bowdrie brothers are the most eligible bachelors in the county, but neither of them have shown any signs of being seriously interested in a woman until you.''

"But, Becky,'' Victoria protested, slightly dazed, "I've only danced with Quinn twice and talked to him a couple of times away from the Crossroads. Why would anyone jump to the conclusion that he's seriously interested in me?''

"Because that's four times more than he's ever bothered to single out any other woman in the county.''

"That's unbelievable. Lonna told me that Quinn rarely dates, but I didn't think—''

"It's closer to the truth to say that Quinn *never* dates,'' Becky interrupted. She waved one hand in the air dismissively. "Oh, I'm not saying that he has no contact with women. Cully teases him about some divorcee he visits now and then in the next county, but as far as taking a woman to dinner or the movies—he simply doesn't.''

"But why not?''

Becky shrugged. "Darned if I know. He was engaged for a short while when he was away at college but broke it off before he came home.''

"What happened?" Victoria asked, curious.

"Don't know. He never talks about it."

"Mmm." Victoria wished Becky had asked him because her instincts told her that the broken engagement was an important piece necessary to the solving of the puzzle that was Quinn. The older woman had been blunt about her loyalty to the Bowdrie brothers, and Victoria was convinced that Becky genuinely cared about Quinn. She decided to return Becky's bluntness with her own. She glanced around the cafe and found that the other diners had lost interest in her.

"I'm going to be honest with you, Becky." The wiry little woman edged forward in her chair, eyeing her expectantly. "I'm…interested…in getting to know Quinn better, but he told me in no uncertain terms that we won't be seeing each other because a connection with him will inevitably destroy my reputation in Colson."

"He's probably right."

Becky's words dashed Victoria's hopes. She'd expected an adamant denial.

"The gossips will have a field day at first," Becky went on. "But they'll get bored and move on to the next juicy tidbit soon enough. If you want Quinn, that's a gamble you'll have to take." Becky's mouth firmed and she frowned at Victoria. "Who do you care most about, girl, Quinn or the local gossips?"

"I've never dealt with small town gossips before," Victoria admitted. "But in the office, I've always dealt with gossips and rumors by simply ignoring them."

"Good." Becky nodded with satisfaction.

"Of course, all of this may be moot," Victoria said thoughtfully. "There's always the possibility that Quinn was letting me down easy and that the real reason he doesn't want to see me is that he simply isn't interested."

"Hah," Becky snorted. "I've never heard that Quinn Bowdrie lost so much as a single night's sleep over a woman. But you've got him so stirred up that Cully's threatening to move out of the main house and pitch a tent in the yard because Quinn's impossible to live with. Don't you worry about whether or not he's interested. In fact, I think it's downright encouraging that he's worried about your reputation. That's a good sign."

"You think so, huh?" Victoria grinned at the little old lady.

"I know so." Becky slapped her palms against the tabletop and pushed to her feet. She slung her handbag over her forearm and fixed Victoria with a stern eye. "You do something about that boy. You hear?"

"Yes, ma'am," Victoria responded solemnly, struggling to keep from smiling. "I will."

"Good. See that you do. You come on out to

the ranch and have lunch with me tomorrow. We'll talk about it.''

"All right." Victoria agreed.

"Come early, before it gets too hot."

After Becky had left the diner, Victoria turned back to her half-eaten salad and cooling coffee. Not that she was inexperienced, but she wasn't at all sure that she could charm Quinn into believing in himself. She wasn't even sure she knew where to start, even if she could get past his determination to save her reputation by staying away from her.

Shortly before noon the next day, Victoria left the outskirts of Colson behind, the two-lane blacktop stretching ahead of her with only an occasional passing car or truck to break the isolation. Barbed wire fences paralleled the road and beyond their barrier, Victoria caught an occasional glimpse of cattle grazing in pastures. Tilled fields broke the monotony of rough terrain with neat sections of spring-green wheat. The land of plains and buttes surrounding Colson had been wheat and cattle country since the turn of the century. Only in the flats along the riverbanks did the occasional rancher's truck garden boast a green lushness from irrigation.

Victoria checked her mileage and fumbled on the seat beside her to find the scribbled note with the directions Becky had dictated over the phone that morning.

The road curved, climbing slightly as it rounded the base of a flat-topped butte, then straightened again, the crossroads no longer visible in Victoria's rearview mirror. Her sense of isolation grew, her car the only sign of human occupation. The empty gravel road stretched ahead of her while behind her, a plume of dust rose from her tires, hanging in the air before slowly dissipating.

Victoria glanced at her mileage gauge, again, wondering if she'd missed the mailboxes and gone too far, when she spotted a lane leading inland from the road just ahead. A large rural mailbox sat atop a sturdy post at the edge of the road, and she slowed to a crawl to read the block letters, painted in black on the gray box.

"Bowdrie." The graded gravel lane curved away from the main road but then it, too, disappeared around the base of a butte. She had no idea how far the ranch buildings were from the main road and she resisted the temptation to drive down the lane to find out. Instead, she accelerated to a fifteen-mile-an-hour crawl, looking for Becky's lane. The car crested the rise of a small hill and below her was another mailbox, black this time, standing guard at the junction of lane and gravel road.

"This must be Becky," she murmured, nodding with satisfaction when she read the gold block letters spelling out B. Sprackett on the big box.

The Sprackett ranch buildings were visible from the road. Victoria pulled up in front of the neat, two-story white house and got out, glancing around her at the well-kept barn, corrals, and several smaller outbuildings.

Her knock on the screen door was answered with a frenzy of barks. She peered through the screen just as a collie threw herself against the door, the racket from her frenzied barking deafening. Startled, Victoria jumped back, wary of the noisy animal, but the door proved a solid barrier between her and the dog and she inched warily closer once more.

"Becky?" she called. If the older woman heard her above the loud barking, she didn't respond. Victoria tried again, louder this time. "Becky!"

The dog grew more agitated, barking louder, but still Becky didn't appear. Victoria eyed the collie.

"What is it, girl? Is something wrong?"

The dog whined frantically, dropped to all fours and barked sharply.

"All right. I'm coming in—but you'd better not bite me."

Victoria cautiously eased the screen door open

a crack, ready to slam it shut if the dog attacked, but the collie only barked again and took two dancing steps down the hall away from her.

Convinced that the dog was trying to tell her something was wrong, Victoria pulled the door open all the way and stepped into the hallway.

"Becky? Becky, are you here?"

No response. Uneasily, Victoria looked at the dog.

"Okay, girl, where is she?"

The collie barked once more and raced down the hallway, disappearing through a door at the far end. Victoria followed her and stepped into the kitchen. One swift, searching glance told her why the dog was frantic.

"Oh, no!" She ran across the room and dropped to her knees beside Becky's slight figure, crumpled motionless on the gleaming linoleum floor. The collie sat on her haunches beside her mistress and whined anxiously. Victoria pressed her fingers against the soft skin of Becky's wrist, sighing with relief when she felt a pulse. "Thank goodness," she murmured.

Her gaze flicked over the older woman's prone figure. A small blue scatter rug, crumpled as if shoved out of the way, lay just beyond her feet.

"Becky—" Victoria brushed a soft strand of gray hair away from her cheek. "Becky, can you hear me?"

She was answered by a soft moan. The worried collie nudged her nose against Becky's outstretched hand.

"Becky—are you awake?"

Blue-veined lids flickered, then lifted slowly to reveal blue eyes filled with confusion.

"Victoria?"

"Yes, Becky, I'm here. Can you tell me what happened?"

"What happened?" she repeated, clearly disoriented.

"You're lying on the floor. Can you tell me what happened? Do you hurt anywhere?"

Awareness crept into the blue gaze, accompanied by pain. Becky grimaced and lifted a shaky hand to touch the back of her head.

"I tripped on the rug and wrenched my ankle. I must have hit my head when I went down because it hurts like the devil. Almost as much as my ankle," she added with weak humor.

"Don't move," Victoria instructed, slipping her fingers in careful exploration up the back of Becky's neck and skull. "I'm going to call the paramedics. Where's the phone, Becky?"

"On the wall—by the refrigerator. But don't bother with the ambulance people. I'm sure I only sprained my ankle and don't need them. Just call Quinn and he'll take me to the hospital. His number is on the pad next to the phone."

The older woman's voice was thready, her refusal to consider that her fall may have done real damage underlaid with worry.

"I'll call both Quinn and the emergency staff," Victoria said gently but firmly. "That way, we'll have all our bases covered, just in case."

"All right."

Concerned, Victoria rose quickly and located the phone. The necessary information was taken quickly and efficiently by the paramedic team and she quickly punched in the numbers for the Bowdrie residence. The phone rang ten times before it was picked up.

"Yeah?"

"Quinn?" Victoria was pretty sure the impatient male voice belonged to Quinn, but it might be Cully.

"Victoria?"

"Hi." Relief flooded her at the sound of his deep voice. "Quinn, I'm so glad I reached you. I'm calling from Becky's house. There's been an accident."

"Is she hurt?"

"Yes—her ankle is either badly sprained or broken and she hit her head when she fell."

"I'll be right there."

Quinn hung up before Victoria could say any more.

Reassured that both Quinn and the ambulance

were on their way, she dropped to her knees beside Becky once again.

"Is my ankle broken?" Becky asked, eyes closed.

"I don't know," Victoria said honestly.

"Mmm." Becky turned her head toward her, wincing as she did.

"I'm going to get you a pillow—and a blanket." Victoria patted her shoulder comfortingly. "Where are they?"

"Linen closet—down the hall by the bathroom."

Victoria jumped up, hurrying out of the room. She didn't like the breathy quality in Becky's voice and wished she remembered more from the first-aid classes she'd taken in college.

Becky lay just as she'd left her. Victoria spread the blanket over her and carefully lifted her head, tucking the pillow beneath.

"There you go," she murmured, smoothing a hand across Becky's brow. "Are you warm enough?"

"Yes, I'm fine." Becky's lashes lifted. "This wasn't exactly what I'd planned for lunch."

"Don't give it another thought," Victoria reassured her. "If you were fated to fall today, I'm glad we made plans, otherwise I wouldn't have found you."

"True."

Becky's lashes drifted lower, as if they were too heavy for her to hold up, and she closed her eyes again. Victoria cast a quick glance at the wall clock.

Ten minutes since I called Quinn and the paramedics. She glanced at Becky's pale face, her features drawn with lines of pain. *Hurry.*

Her plea was answered by the growl of a truck engine.

"Thank goodness," she murmured.

A truck door slammed, boots thudded across the porch, and the screen door squeaked open.

"Victoria?"

The sound of Quinn's deep voice flooded her with relief.

"We're in the kitchen."

Quinn's long strides carried him quickly down the hall and into the kitchen. One swift glance took in Becky's crumpled figure. Victoria knelt beside her, worry etching her features.

"Hey, Becky." He dropped to one knee on the kitchen floor next to her, his voice gently teasing. "What have you been up to?"

Becky managed a wan smile.

"Nothing good, I'm afraid. I tripped over that darn rug and twisted my ankle."

Victoria listened as Quinn quietly soothed the injured Becky, glancing at the kitchen clock every few moments. It was another fifteen minutes, however, before she heard the sound of a vehicle outside.

"That must be the paramedics, Quinn," she murmured softly. "I'll let them in."

"Mmm?" Becky stirred.

"Shh." Quinn calmed her. "The EMTs are here."

Victoria rose and hurried down the hall to the front door.

"Hello." She pushed open the door for the two uniformed men climbing the porch steps. "I'm so glad to see you."

"Where's Becky?" the older one asked as he eased past her, bag in hand.

"She's in the kitchen—straight down the hall and through the door to your left."

"Mrs. Sprackett?"

Becky's eyes opened, and she peered up at the young man bending over her.

"What happened?" The older man wrapped a blood pressure cuff around her arm and began to pump, watching the gauge.

"I tripped—fell on the rug in front of the sink. If it hadn't been for Victoria, who knows how long I'd have lain here before you were called. Probably not until Quinn came by and found me." Becky shifted, wincing."

"Don't move, Becky," the older paramedic ordered. "I don't think the ankle's broken, but we need to keep you still. And we should have it X-rayed. You've got one heck of a sprain there,'' he continued, extracting a roll of elastic bandage. He began to wrap her ankle. ''You'll have to stay off this foot for a while.''

''How long?''

''At least a week, maybe two. When we get to the hospital, the doctor can probably give you a better time frame.''

''I'm not going to the hospital,'' Becky said firmly.

''Now, Becky—'' the older paramedic began patiently.

''Don't you 'now, Becky' me,'' she snapped. ''I don't want to go to the hospital and that's that!''

''But you can't stay here alone. That ankle won't get better unless you stay off of it completely and that means total bed rest.''

''Give me a cane. I'll hobble around and won't use my foot and ankle.''

''I don't think the doctor would approve of your being out of bed, not even if you used a cane.''

Becky glowered at him.

''What if I stayed here with her?'' Victoria suggested. ''Granted, I don't have any nursing experience, but if all she needs is someone to make sure she doesn't need to get out of bed...''

Becky beamed at Victoria, her pale face brightening.

"There, you see." Triumphant, she turned to the paramedic. "I won't be alone."

"Can you be here twenty-four hours a day?" the man asked, eyeing Victoria doubtfully.

"I don't see why not."

"What about your job at the pharmacy and the law office?" Quinn asked.

"I'll call my uncle and let him know what happened. If he needs help, Aunt Sheila can cover for me."

Quinn, Victoria and Becky all looked at the paramedic.

He shrugged. "It's up to you. You should still have your ankle X-rayed, Becky, and call your own physician to have him check you over. We'll make sure he gets copies of our report, but he'll most likely want to see you in his office."

"I'll drive her to Colson to her doctor's office," Quinn told the medic. "He can take X rays and examine her."

The medic nodded and snapped his bag shut.

"Fine." Becky glanced at Quinn. "If you'll give me a hand, Quinn, I'll hobble out to your truck."

"You aren't going to hobble anywhere," he told her firmly as he knelt to slip his arms under her legs and shoulders. "Wrap your arms around my neck."

Becky obeyed and he stood, lifting her carefully. She moaned softly when her foot left the support of the folded rug. Upright, Quinn paused. "All right?"

"Fine."

Quinn looked at Victoria. "Do you want to come with us?"

"Of course."

Three hours later, Victoria carefully pulled the bedroom door closed and tiptoed down the stairs. Quinn rose from a chair on the porch and held the screen door for her.

"How's she doing?"

"She's asleep. Poor thing—she's exhausted."

"Yeah. I never think of Becky as being elderly. Seeing her crumpled up on the floor like that was a shock."

"I know—for me, too."

Quinn glanced sideways at her. Her eyes were solemn, and he fought the urge to pull her into his arms.

"Thanks for offering to stay with Becky—and for going to Dr. Anders's office with us. She's scared to death of hospitals—always said that all they're good for is a place for old folks to die. It means a lot to her to have you here—and to me, too.''

"I'm glad that I can be of help." Victoria was deeply touched by his concern for Becky's fear. Clearly, Becky's affection for Quinn wasn't one-sided. "You don't have to thank me, Quinn."

"Yeah, well…" His voice was rough with emotion. He tugged his Stetson lower over his brow and cleared his throat. "I'd better go. I have some things I need to get done at home so I can be back here in time to do Becky's evening chores. Do you want me to run into town and pick up Becky's medicine?"

"No, I need to call Lonna and have her stop by my apartment to collect some clothes for the next couple of weeks. She can drop by the pharmacy to pick up the pain medication and bring it out with her."

"All right. Either Cully or I will stay near a phone this afternoon. Don't hesitate to call if you need anything." He didn't wait for a response. Instead, he touched the brim of his Stetson in goodbye and left her.

She stood on the porch, watching as his truck pulled away, before she turned back into the house.

The first few days and nights were difficult. Despite the pain medication, Becky's ankle throbbed and plagued her. She slept in fits and starts, and Victoria was kept busy running up and down the stairs to Becky's second-floor bedroom during the day. Reluctant to leave the older woman awake and alone in the night, Victoria kept a book on the nightstand to read aloud from in the long hours between midnight and dawn. When she wasn't tending to Becky during the day, she snatched what sleep she could and as a result, she saw little of Quinn.

The third night, Becky fell asleep at ten o'clock and Victoria climbed into her own bed, exhausted. She woke just before dawn, her lashes lifting slowly. A vague feeling of uneasiness swept her and she frowned, staring at the ceiling over her bed. Something was wrong.

Comprehension dawned as she realized the significance of waking in her own bed.

Becky slept through the night.

Relieved, Victoria stretched, curling her toes against smooth cotton sheets. A small smile of satisfaction curved her mouth, and she turned her head on the pillow. Outside the window, dark night had lightened to a predawn gray that was quickly brightening as the sun peeked over the horizon.

Unable to go back to sleep, Victoria got up and headed downstairs. Early-morning sunshine poured through the kitchen windows. Operating on automatic pilot, Victoria went through the motions of measuring coffee and water, then switched on the coffeemaker.

Annie nudged her cold nose against Victoria's palm.

"Hmm. What is it, girl?"

The dog padded to the door and looked expectantly back over her shoulder.

"Oh, you want out." Victoria obligingly let the dog go ahead of her across the utility porch, then unlocked and held open the outside door. Annie whisked past her and out into the morning sunshine.

Victoria squinted against the intrusion of light and pulled the door shut, wending her way back into the kitchen to lean against the counter, stare unfocused at the coffeemaker and pray that the brew finished perking sooner rather than later.

"Good morning, sunshine."

The male voice was deep and filled with amusement. Startled, Victoria's sluggish heart slammed into overdrive.

She whirled to face the room, the knee-length skirt of her robe lifting, swirling around her thighs before settling once more.

Quinn stood just inside the door leading to the utility room, holding a large galvanized pail filled with foamy milk.

"What are..." She gulped, one hand pressed

over her galloping heart. "What are you doing here? You scared me to death!"

"Sorry. I thought you heard me come in the back door."

"Well, I didn't." She frowned at him. "You're disgustingly cheerful."

He quirked an eyebrow and grinned. "And you're grumpy. Are you always cranky when you first wake up?"

"Yes." The grin lightened his features, the sight inflicting another jolt to Victoria's sluggish heart. The coffeemaker behind her beeped, and she sighed with relief. "Thank goodness."

She turned her back on Quinn and opened the cupboard to take down two mugs. She filled them and handed one to Quinn, cradling her own in her palms and leaning against the counter while she sipped. The coffee was hot, black and strong.

Quinn headed for the utility porch.

"Where are you going?" Victoria asked.

He lifted the pail and paused to glance at her. "I have to process Becky's milk. By the time the coffee wakes you up, I'll be back."

Satisfied that he wasn't leaving, Victoria returned to her coffee, absentmindedly noting what sounded like pans rattling in the utility room, then the hum of a motor.

When Quinn reentered the kitchen ten minutes later, she felt almost human.

"Want some more coffee?" she asked, refilling her own cup.

"Sure." Quinn washed and dried his hands at the sink, then leaned an elbow on the countertop beside her. "So, how many gallons of coffee does it take to get you going in the morning?" he asked, his tone curious.

"Go sit down," she told him. "I'm not awake enough to deal with you." She pushed the steaming mug into his hand. "Shoo."

He laughed and did as he was told, depositing his mug on the tabletop before he pulled out a chair and sat, his long legs stretched out, booted feet crossed at the ankle.

Victoria picked up her own cup and started for the table. She stumbled over his boots. With one quick move, Quinn lifted her mug from her hand, set it on the table and wrapped his arm around her waist to steady her.

She responded by losing her balance entirely and tumbling into his lap.

Before she could catch her breath, his arms trapped her neatly. She blinked and frowned at him.

"What do you think you're doing?" she demanded.

He lifted a brow and eyed her. "What do I think *I'm* doing? You're the one who threw yourself at me."

"That's a lie. Your feet were in my way and I stumbled," she said without heat. His body was solid and warm beneath her, his arms holding her securely. She stifled a yawn and blinked at him. His green gaze watched her intently, a slight, bemused curve to his hard mouth. "This isn't funny," she commented. "And the minute I wake up, I'll get off your lap and we'll discuss it."

"Fine."

He shifted, his arms tightening.

"What are you doing?"

"Cuddling you." He cradled her cheek in the palm of one hand and gently pushed her head down to lie on his shoulder. "Until you wake up."

"Oh." The strong, rhythmic thump of his heartbeat beneath her cheek was oddly comforting. She smoothed her palm over his shirt just below his collarbone. "I'll argue with you about that later."

"All right," he replied easily.

Silence reigned in the kitchen. Quinn leaned forward and picked up his mug, then eased back to cradle her close once again while he sipped his coffee.

"Becky must have had a good night," Victoria murmured. "She didn't wake me even once."

"Good." He bent his head. "So you slept the night through?"

"Yes. Becky's still asleep, but I'm so used to the alarm going off at five a.m. for work in Seattle that I automatically woke at five this morning."

"Why didn't you just roll over and go back to sleep?"

"I tried. It didn't work. I finally gave up, got out of bed and dragged myself down here to make coffee. Speaking of which—" she lifted her head, snagged his mug from his fingers and drank "—Mmm." She pushed the cup back into his hand and returned her cheek to the comfort of his chest. "You make a good pillow." She said sleepily.

"Hmm. You know," he said reflectively. "A man could get used to this."

"Used to what?"

"Drinking his morning coffee with a half-naked woman on his lap."

"I'm not half-naked."

"No? Darn." He said mildly. "I could have sworn you aren't wearing a bra."

Victoria didn't rise to the bait. Instead, she flexed her fingers, her nails threatening the hard muscle beneath cotton. "And I could have sworn you wouldn't take advantage of me when I'm still two-thirds asleep."

"Ouch." Quinn slid his mug onto the table and caught her fingers in his, carefully removing them from his shirt. "You've got sharp claws, woman."

"Mmm." She wasn't sure if it was the caffeine coursing through her bloodstream or the banter with Quinn, but Victoria was definitely starting to wake up. She peered at him through half-lowered lashes. "The better to scratch you with, my dear."

"Haven't you got that backward? I'm the wolf—and that would make you Little Red Riding Hood."

Victoria plucked at the skirt of her apple-green cotton robe. "Wrong color."

"I'll make allowances."

The quiet was broken by a sharp bark, followed by the scratch of nails against the back door.

Quinn glanced at his watch.

"Much as I hate to leave you, sweetheart, I have to get going." He eased her off his lap and stood. "I'll let Annie in on my way out."

"Thanks."

He tipped her chin up, brushed warm lips against hers and gently tapped the tip of her nose with his forefinger.

"I definitely could get used to this. How about breakfast with my coffee tomorrow morning?"

"I'll think about it."

"You do that."

He left the kitchen. Seconds later, Annie

bounded into the kitchen. She nudged her nose under Victoria's palm in a bid for attention.

"Morning, girl." Victoria bent to rub the collie's silky ears. "Sorry, I was distracted by Quinn. I bet you want breakfast, don't you?"

Annie's ears pricked with interest. Panting, she gave Victoria her version of a doggy grin.

The memory of sharing the early-morning quiet with Quinn stayed with Victoria and she found herself smiling at odd hours throughout the day.

Chapter Five

Having coffee and breakfast with Quinn became
a habit over the next few days. He arrived each
morning just after dawn to milk Becky's cow,
feed her chickens and fork hay down to the
horses. Since Victoria's internal clock continued
to go off precisely at five every morning, she rose,
dressed and had breakfast ready when Quinn
brought the milk to the house. He teased her about
being domestic, she blithely threatened him with
legal action and was pleasantly surprised when he
didn't react with stiffness and anger to the casual
reminder of her profession.

Becky grew increasingly impatient with her forced hours in bed. Still, the doctor adamantly refused to give her permission to use a cane and hobble around the house.

The days fell into a routine, the hours drifting slowly one into another. Surprisingly, Victoria didn't grow bored with the quiet rhythm. One afternoon toward the end of the second week, she left Becky napping upstairs and wandered outside to wash her car. The thermometer hovered in the low-80's, Annie lay in the shade at the end of the porch, stretched out against the cool board floor. Two horses stood at the far end of the corral, deep in the shadow cast by the barn roof, heads down, tails swishing sporadically at bottleflies.

Annie stirred, lifting her head from her paws when Victoria poked around at the base of the porch, searching for the faucet.

"Ah-ha. Here you are." Tucked behind tall snapdragons, the faucet had a hose already attached. Victoria collected the spray nozzle hooked over the metal pipe and followed the green vinyl around the corner of the house. A sprinkler was attached to the far end. She disconnected it, twisted the nozzle on in its place, and towed the long hose after her to the sidewalk and out the gate to the car before returning to the house. She ran lightly up the stairs, pausing to peek in on the still sleeping Becky, before tiptoeing quietly down the hall to her bedroom to change into a pair of cutoffs and a white, bra-cut top. Quick brush strokes swept her hair into a ponytail and a few swift twists of a ribbon band secured the silky mane high above her nape. A quick stop in the kitchen located a pail, soap, old towels and a brush to scrub the car's wheels.

She hung the towels over one of the gate's pickets, dumped soap into the pail, and ran water over the granules. The sun was hot on her bare shoulders, legs, midriff and scalp.

More wet than dry, she was bent over, scrubbing the hood of the car, when Quinn drove in a half hour later.

She pushed upright, a hand raised to shade her eyes, and watched him climb out of the truck and walk toward her.

"Hi." She smiled, delighted to see him. "You've got perfect timing, Bowdrie. I was just about to scrub the wheels, but since you're here…"

Hands on hips, he looked her up and down, quick heat flaring in his eyes. "Damn, Denning. You're soaking wet."

She held her arms away from her body, one hand clutching a torn hand towel that dripped soap suds onto the ground, and looked down. The sun top and faded jean cutoffs were damp down the front, the result of leaning against the wet car body while she stretched to reach across the roof of the car. The cutoffs were soaked over her hips where she'd rubbed her hands in an effort to dry them, and her toes curled against the wet leather of her sandals.

"You're right." She agreed cheerfully, brushing her forearm across her cheek in a vain attempt to push a tendril of hair out of her eyes. "I'm drenched." She tipped her face up to the sun. "Not a bad thing to be in this heat. You should try it, Quinn."

"No, thanks." He said dryly. "I'm not dressed for it."

"So, how about it? Are you going to scrub the wheels?"

"All right. Where's the brush?"

"Right here." She fished the scrub brush from the bottom of the pail and tossed it to him. Too late, she realized that an arc of soap bubbles and water drops trailed the brush's flight.

Quinn caught the wet brush one-handed and shook his head at her.

"I *don't* want to get wet," he warned.

"Oops, sorry." She walked around the car, dragging the hose, and sprayed the wheel wells. "There's a can of cleanser by the gate."

Quinn rounded the hood of the car, staying well away from the hose spray, and collected the can. He waited until Victoria returned to scrubbing the hood before he went down on his haunches on the far side of the car.

"You're here early for evening chores," Victoria commented.

"I took the afternoon off."

His voice was muffled, Victoria glanced up but couldn't see him above the car body.

"Now there's a first," she said with amusement. "I didn't know ranchers ever took a day off."

"I didn't take a day off, just the afternoon and evening. Cully's doing the chores at home tonight." He stretched to reach the far side of the tire, his boots slipping in the wet dirt that was fast turning into mud. "Hell," he muttered, catching himself just in time to keep from landing on his rear in a puddle.

"What was that?"

"Nothing." Quinn said, louder. He could tell from the sound of her voice that she was on the far side of the car. Finished with the tire and its chrome rim, he shifted, without standing up, the few feet necessary to reach the next tire on that side.

Two seconds later, a waterfall swept over the hood of the car and poured over him.

"Hey!" He shot to his feet.

"Oh, no!" Stunned, Victoria stared at him for a full second, water continuing to arc between

them, before she remembered to take her thumb
from the nozzle handle. The spray from the hose
shut off immediately, but water continued to drip
from the brim of Quinn's hat, running down his
face to slide off his jaw. A jaw that was hard as
granite. Her gaze raced to meet his and found his
green eyes narrowed, threatening. "Oh, Quinn!
I'm sorry, I really am." She waved the hand holding the hose toward the rear of the car. "I thought
you were washing the rear tire. I swear I didn't
know you were there. Honest."

Quinn slowly lifted a hand and drew it down
his face, sluicing water from his skin. He pulled
off his hat and looked at the wet spots.

"You got my hat wet. My good hat."

"I'm sorry." Victoria surmised that she'd com-
mitted a cardinal sin. "Is it ruined?"

"No, it's not ruined. But it's wet."

Clearly, that made sense to him. It didn't to
Victoria, but then, she wasn't in any position to
argue. "Can we dry it?" She asked tentatively.

He glowered at her and splashed through the
muddy puddles to the gate where he hung the hat
on one of the pickets, then stripped off his wet
shirt and tossed it over the gate. He leaned against
the post and tugged off his boots and socks before
he strode around the car to Victoria.

She discovered that a half-wet, half-naked, irritated male was intimidating. He stopped in front

of her and held out his hand. She looked at his open palm.

"What?"

"Give me the hose. You're dangerous with that thing."

Meekly, she held out the hose, then snatched it back. "Wait a minute. I'm not giving you this hose unless you promise not to spray me," she said stoutly.

"I won't spray you," he growled.

She handed him the hose.

"At least, not this minute."

Too late. Victoria watched a wicked grin curve his mouth and realized she'd been had.

"Don't even think about it, Quinn," she warned.

Hot sun gleamed off the satiny skin of his bare shoulders, sleek muscles flexed and shifted as he stepped toward her.

She backed up. One step. Two. His thumb flicked the nozzle hammer and spray settled over her in a cold stream. She shrieked and ducked away, brought up short against the car fender.

The spray stopped as abruptly as it had begun. Victoria leaned against the car, blinking. Drops of water clung to her lashes. She ran her fingertips over her closed lashes and down her cheeks, wiping away water. The chilly water left goose bumps on her arms and she held her hands wide, looking down at the damage.

If she'd been damp before, now she was truly drenched. She lifted her head, expecting to find Quinn laughing at her.

He wasn't laughing.

His gaze was fastened on her breasts.

Victoria already knew the shock of cold water had puckered her nipples, drawing them tight against the soft cotton of her wet sun top. They rucked tighter under Quinn's stare, and heat chased the last of the goose bumps from her skin.

He dropped the hose to the ground, his slow strides predatory as he closed the distance between them.

"Quinn?" Her voice faltered, unsure, vaguely threatened.

"Victoria."

Just her name, only her name. But his husky, deep voice carried a wealth of passion, need and reassurance. The instinctive female wariness within her, threatened by the sexually aroused male in Quinn, calmed and disappeared under a wave of heated excitement. Her head tilted back, her lashes lowering.

He gripped her waist and lifted her to sit on the wet fender, dropping his head to nuzzle the sensitive skin at the base of her throat where her pulse throbbed frantically. His hands brushed up the side of her ribcage and found her breasts, palming them with careful, barely controlled fierceness. His thumbs moved restlessly over the wet cloth covering her nipples, each stroke stealing her breath and forcing her heartbeat ever faster.

"Quinn." She murmured. Her fingers clutched his shoulders, the sleek muscles taut, his satiny skin hot from the sun's rays without and the desire that raged within.

He pushed her knees apart and wedged between, one hand cradling her bottom to pull her forward, flush against his jeans, just as his lips deserted her throat for her mouth.

Victoria was assaulted with heat. Beneath her hands, the satiny skin of his shoulders was burning. Against her midriff, flush with his, bare skin pressed against, shifted, and heated bare skin. Beneath the ragged edge of her cutoff jeans and against her sensitive inner thighs, worn denim rubbed gently against soft skin. His mouth was fused to hers, demanding, luring, seducing.

She wanted more. Much more. Frantic to get closer, she wrapped her legs around him, her calves rubbing the backs of his thighs.

He groaned, his hips pressing hard against her for a moment before he ripped his mouth from hers and dropped his head to her shoulder. His breath came in short, hard pants.

Victoria fought to catch her breath. Pressed tight against him, each labored breath she drew in carried the scent of soap and musky male. His body was strung taut, the muscles in his powerful arms corded, faint tremors shaking him as he fought for control.

"We can't keep doing this," he rasped, lifting his head to look at her. "It's driving me crazy. Sooner or later, I won't be able to stop."

"I don't want you to stop." The words were out before she had time to consider them. They hung in the air, charging the space between them with tension so thick it seemed to pulse.

"Do you know what you're saying?"

Guttural, the words were so low she could barely hear them, yet they pounded in her brain. The skin was drawn tight over his face, flushed cheekbones streaked with color, heavy-lidded eyes dark with arousal.

"Yes. No." Frustrated, she shook her head. "I want you. Badly. But I never meant for this— us—to go this far."

"I warned you. I told you that I don't do relationships."

"I know." Her gaze searched his. "And I don't do affairs. Where does that leave us, Quinn?"

"Hell." He closed his eyes and dropped his head back, sucking in a deep breath and releasing it before he looked at her. "I don't know."

"I don't know, either," she confessed. "I don't want to stop seeing you, Quinn. I like you."

His eyes narrowed. "I like you, too. I'd like you better after a couple of days in bed. Maybe we'd burn this out of our systems."

"You think so?"

The interest and curiosity in her expression brought a reluctant laugh to his lips. "Maybe, I don't know."

"I'm not ready to go to bed with you, Quinn."

His mouth twisted in an almost-smile, the full lower lip sensual.

"You damn sure feel ready."

Victoria flushed. She couldn't deny that she wanted him so badly she burned with frustration. "That's my body talking, not my brain."

"Sweetheart," he murmured. "It's your body I want, not your brain."

She stiffened, and he tugged the damp end of her ponytail.

"Easy, honey, I'm just being honest. Everything about your body turns me on, from this cute little ponytail to the girly pink paint on your toenails. But I have to admit that I like your brain, too."

Her poker-stiff spine relaxed, but only a fraction.

"You do? Why?" Her voice was suspicious.

"Because you're the first woman I've met

who's smart, funny, kind to old ladies and dogs, all wrapped up in one very sexy package. So, yeah, I guess your brain is part of the appeal.''

Mollified and secretly pleased by his words, Victoria's back loosened and she relaxed against him.

"So what are we going to do about this?"

He sighed, deeply. "Nothing. Even if you were ready and willing, Becky's upstairs and will probably be awake soon. Then there's your uncle."

"My uncle?"

"I owe him. It seems downright traitorous to repay him by taking his niece to bed." He smiled at her. "Becky tells me that your aunt and uncle think the sun rises and sets in you. They're as proud of you as they are of Lonna."

"That's nice to know. It's mutual," she added, his words warming her heart. "I think they're pretty terrific, too."

"Yeah." Reluctantly, he stepped back from her. He propped his fists on the polished red metal, his arms caging her without touching her, and trapped her gaze with his intent stare. "There's no wiggle room. None. So that means no more running around in wet scanty tops and bare legs, okay?"

"This top isn't scanty." Her protest was automatic.

"Right." He flicked a quick, skeptical glance

down her body and back up again to meet hers. "Try wearing one of those black gowns and veils women wear in Kuwait. I might be able to keep my hands off you if you're smothered in heavy black material."

Victoria laughed.

"In this heat? I don't think so."

"Somehow I knew you weren't going to co-operate." He caught her waist and swung her to the ground. "Let's finish washing your car." He fixed her with a steely gaze. "And *do not* turn that damned hose on me again."

"Yes, Quinn."

He left her, shaking his head and muttering, and headed around the car to finish scrubbing wheels. Victoria returned to sloshing water over the driver's side door and scrubbing determinedly.

Later that evening, dinner finished and Becky contentedly watching a mystery on the television upstairs, Quinn and Victoria carried their coffee mugs outside to the porch. They bypassed the rocking chairs and chose to sit on the edge of the porch, feet stretched out across the shallow steps.

"You sit over there," Quinn instructed. "And don't come any closer than three feet."

"Truce." Victoria turned to face him, her back against the post, her legs angled companionably across the step toward his.

The sun dipped toward the horizon and slipped below, streaking the sky with bands of gold and pink, painting the underbellies of puffy white clouds with color. Dusk began to creep across the land, long shadows inching toward the two seated on the steps.

The scent of roses, blooming in the flower beds edging the porch, lay heavy on the warm evening air.

"There's something wonderfully peaceful about watching the sun go down over buttes and open prairie," Victoria said softly, almost to herself.

Quinn glanced sideways. She gazed at the horizon, her face in profile. Still, he could read the faint wonder on her features, hear it in her voice.

"Not the same as watching the sun set over city concrete, is it?"

"No." She flashed a quick smile, her gaze meeting his with empathy. "No, it's definitely not the same. Although, to be fair, I've seen some memorable photos that captured sundown, and sunup, on streets in Seattle. There can be a stark kind of beauty in a deserted early-morning street and skyscrapers."

"I suppose."

Dusk deepened around them. Victoria had switched on a lamp when they passed through the living room and it threw a faint bar of light across the porch floorboards. The light filtered through the screen door but didn't quite stretch far enough to reach the steps.

"Do you miss it?" he asked.

Victoria's gaze left the shadowy horizon and found his. "What? The city?"

"The city—and your life there." He gestured at the darkened landscape. "This is quite a change from urban living."

"Yes, it is," she agreed, falling silent as she considered his words. "I do miss my brothers and my parents. And my work. And double lattes and shopping in downtown Seattle. But oddly enough," she added slowly, slightly startled by the realization, "I'm not unhappy here. Even though initially I couldn't imagine not practicing law for six months, I was determined to get well. Then I moved to Colson and after the first few weeks of gearing down, it hasn't been nearly as bad as I'd imagined." She chuckled softly. "Not that it's been easy, but there's something to be said for actually having the time to watch the sun go down."

"What? The sun doesn't set in Seattle?" he teased.

"Of course it does. I just didn't get to see it very often."

"Why not?"

"Because I rarely left my office before nine or

ten. Even if I'd rated an office with a window, I was so buried in work I doubt that I would have taken time to watch the sun go down.''

"You worked until ten at night? What time did you start in the morning?''

"My alarm went off at five. I normally was in my office and working by six-thirty.''

Quinn's brows lifted in disbelief.

"That's a hell of a long day. What about weekends?''

"They were pretty much the same, although I ate my cereal and read the paper in bed until seven, then went jogging and picked up a latte at the local coffee bar before work. The nice thing about weekends was that I got to wear jeans to work instead of a suit.''

"You worked seven days a week?''

"Yes.''

"That's ridiculous.''

"Probably.'' Victoria couldn't disagree. Her work schedule had been exhausting. "But it was the same for all the attorneys new to the firm. After a few years and a couple of promotions, I might have been able to cut back to six days a week and make it home by seven or eight at night.''

"And you liked this?'' he demanded, baffled. One thing was glaringly apparent—she couldn't have had time for much of a social life.

"I got tired of it sometimes, but my goal was to make partner in ten years. That meant I had to work hard."

"That's not working hard," he said bluntly. "That's slave labor. What about a life outside your work?"

"Now you sound like my father. He and my mother have been asking me that ever since I entered law school."

"So what's your answer?"

Victoria shrugged. "I suppose the only answer is that I didn't have time for a life away from the office."

"What about friends?"

"My friends were the people I worked with and I saw them at work all day. I never felt the need to spend my rare off time with them."

"What about men? And don't tell me guys didn't ask you out."

"I'd go to lunch with one or two of the single male attorneys at the office from time to time. To tell you the truth, I was too tired to look forward to dating very often."

"Yeah, right," he drawled.

A companionable silence stretched between them.

"I guess that means that there isn't some guy waiting for you back in Seattle."

"Sneaky, Quinn. Very sneaky." She leaned toward him, her gaze pinning his. "If you want to know if I'm involved, you should just ask me."

The laughter in her voice irked Quinn.

"All right. I'm asking," he muttered.

"Now was that so hard?"

"Just answer the question."

She chuckled. "No, I'm not involved. In fact, I've only been sort-of involved once. In college. It didn't work out and we parted friends. End of story. Now it's your turn." She eyed him expectantly but he didn't answer. "Come on, Quinn, give. I told you, now you tell me. What about your love life?"

Chapter Six

"You already know about my love life. I don't have one."

"None?" Victoria sipped her coffee, watching him over the rim of her cup. "That's not what Becky told me."

His eyes narrowed. "Becky? What did she tell you?"

"Only that she thought you have a lady friend in the next county—but that it's not serious."

Quinn groaned inwardly. Women. Even Becky gossiped about his sex life.

"How the hell did she find out about that?" he grumbled, embarrassed.

"I think Cully told her."

"I'm going to kill my brother."

"Don't do that. It's not his fault. It's very difficult to tell Becky no if she wants information from a person."

"True."

Victoria waited, but he offered no further comment. "So was Becky right?"

"About what?"

"About the lady in the next county?"

"I see a woman in Hadley every now and then," he confirmed reluctantly. "But not very often. It's been a few months."

"I see." The terse words stabbed Victoria, surprising her. A few months. That was long before she met him and shouldn't affect her one way or the other. But it did. She sipped her coffee and frowned, mulling over her reaction. "And you told me you don't do relationships, so I assume that you've never been married."

"No. Hell, no."

His vehement denial left no room for doubt. Curious, Victoria badly wanted to know if Becky and Lonna's belief that he'd been engaged once were true. Short of bluntly asking him outright, however, which she was reluctant to do, she wasn't sure how to find out.

"So you've never even been close to marriage," she ventured.

Quinn looked away from her, his profile hard as granite. At last, he broke the small silence.

"I was engaged in college."

Victoria glanced at him. The light from the living room softly illuminated the left half of his face, the right side shadowed by the night. His tension was palpable. Even in the dim light, she saw a muscle flex in his jaw.

"What happened?"

"She decided that marriage to me would be hell."

Shocked, Victoria was speechless.

"But… How could she say such a thing?"

"Because it's true." Quinn's gaze left the dark landscape and met hers. "We were good in bed together," he said bluntly. "But when we weren't in bed I didn't talk to her enough, didn't pay enough attention to her. She loved parties and people, but the people she spent time with and the parties she kept dragging me to bored me stiff. To make a long story short, she broke off the engagement. Two weeks later, she married somebody else."

"And it broke your heart," Victoria said softly.

"No. It didn't break my heart. That's the point."

"I don't understand."

"Victoria, I don't have a heart to break. Connie and I were good in bed together, but I just wasn't interested in spending every hour of the day with her after sex.''

"But that doesn't mean you don't have a heart," Victoria protested. "It's not unusual for a man and woman to have a physical connection without an emotional connection. Women's magazines run articles about that subject all the time.''

"Maybe, but a physical connection is all I've ever had. Connie needed more from me than I knew how to give, she wanted me to be in love with her." His brooding gaze met Victoria's. "Whatever the hell that means."

And she hurt you. His fiancée may not have broken Quinn's heart, but it seemed clear that Connie's swift marriage to another man indicated betrayal. When added to the childhood abandonment by his mother and Eileen's battling in court over his father's will, Quinn had more than enough reason to distrust women. With the sole exception of Becky's staunch championship and loyal friendship, Victoria wondered if any female had ever been faithful and good to Quinn. Victoria ached for the guilt and pain she saw in his eyes. "You were both very young, Quinn."

"I was old enough to know that marriage isn't for me. I learned that lesson from my father and mother before I was ten years old," he said grimly. "When Connie left, I promised myself that I wouldn't forget again. Bowdrie men don't make good husbands, Victoria, we don't know how.''

''Did you father actually tell you that?''

''He didn't have to. I was old enough to remember my mother crying for hours before she disappeared. Later, when he took Cully and I to live with him at the ranch, I watched him and Eileen fight on a daily basis. It isn't something I'm likely to forget.''

''But just because your father and stepmother had a bad marriage doesn't mean that you're doomed to suffer the same fate, Quinn.''

''That's a chance I'm not willing to take. I don't want to live with a woman who grows to hate me because I can't love her enough, nor do I plan to father any children and force them to grow up in that hell. Kids deserve a father who can make their mother happy and give them a good life, who'll teach them about family. I can't do that.''

''I think you're wrong, Quinn. You were wonderful with little Bobby at the pharmacy, you knew just what to say to him. I think you'd be a very good father. As for having no heart, no one who's watched you with Becky would ever agree with that statement. You're tender and gentle and obviously care very much for her.''

Her words warmed Quinn's heart, touching him deeply and easing the coldness inside.

"And as for your father," Victoria continued, leaning forward to clasp his forearm. "It seems to me that his actions are a testament that he was an honorable man. Despite the difficulties for himself, he did what he could for you and Cully. He made a home for you, gave you his name and in the end, left you a substantial inheritance. Those aren't the actions of a man who doesn't love, Quinn."

"Maybe." Quinn's hand closed over hers and she immediately turned her palm up to his. He threaded his fingers through hers and stared at their hands, her slim fingers pale against his darker, stronger ones. He wondered if she could possibly be right. "He was a hard man, more comfortable with men than with women or children. He had his own code of honor—all his neighbors will tell you that if he gave his word, he kept it. I respected him, but I can't say I ever really knew him."

"That was his loss," Victoria murmured, struck anew by the lack of warmth and affection in Quinn's life.

Something about her quiet conviction eased the tight band that squeezed Quinn's chest. The tightness always accompanied any mention of his father and was one of the reasons Quinn rarely talked about him.

His gaze searched hers but he found no pity

there. Instead, her blue eyes held understanding, warmth and compassion. For the first time in his life, he'd met a woman that he could laugh with, play with, and share the beauty of a sunset with in companionable silence. An intelligent woman with a wry sense of humor lived within that sinfully sexy package that first attracted him.

Victoria Denning had slipped beneath his defenses and found a place within him he hadn't known existed. If he didn't know it was impossible, he might think that she'd found his heart.

But of course, he reminded himself grimly, he didn't have a heart. At least, not one he'd admit to.

Quinn pushed away his thoughts and refused to give a name to the surge of emotion that swept him. He lifted their clasped hands and brushed his lips across the backs of her fingers.

"I'd better be going. Four in the morning comes too early."

Quinn left and Victoria climbed the stairs to bed. She turned out the lights and slipped between the sheets but sleep wouldn't come. Troubled, she lay awake in the moonlit room, pondering her conversation with Quinn. The dark shadows of night had encouraged intimacy and confessions and she'd felt an elemental shift in her relationship with Quinn. Something had changed between them.

Or perhaps she'd simply been forced to admit the truth.

She could no longer pretend that seeing Quinn was only a way to pass the time while she was in Colson. Nor could she convince herself any longer that she wanted only to repay his gallantry by proving to him that he wasn't the man Eileen Bowdrie claimed.

Something had happened to her the night they met. He'd held out his hand to her on that dance floor and her life hadn't been the same since. The practical side of her brain told her that love at first sight was illogical, but instinct as old as Eve and Adam told her that her fate had been sealed the first time he'd smiled at her and took her hand.

She twisted, punched her pillow in a futile effort to get comfortable and rolled onto her side to stare out the window at the dark night.

Quinn's insistence that he was heartless and incapable of loving was a huge barrier. His belief obviously went bone-deep and that part of him scared her. She thought she'd caught glimpses of the real Quinn over the past several weeks, especially tonight, when he'd opened up and told her things she suspected he rarely spoke about. It was difficult, if not impossible, to glimpse that deeper side of his character and believe that Quinn wasn't capable of an enduring, powerful love.

Still, if she were wrong, she wasn't sure she could accept that all he might ever feel for her was the explosive chemistry between them while she struggled with a much deeper emotional connection.

The man she thought she could safely tease and tempt because he was determined not to seduce her, was suddenly very dangerous.

She had the uneasy feeling that Quinn Bowdrie might be the one man who could break her heart.

What was I thinking? She nearly groaned aloud. *Lonna tried to warn me, but I wouldn't listen.*

She had no idea how to handle her feelings for him. And that scared her. Because Quinn threatened her emotions in ways no man ever had before.

And in a few months, they would be separated by three states and hundreds of miles when she returned to Seattle. Quinn would remain in Montana. Did she really want to complicate her life with a man too far away and too memorable to forget?

And what about Quinn? He'd never denied that he was physically attracted to her, but after the past weeks, Victoria had come to hope that his emotions ran deeper than mere lust. And if he did care for her, how much damage would be done to his already battered, carefully guarded heart if she walked away from him?

Victoria was torn. How could she avoid hurting Quinn and still protect her own vulnerable heart.

It's too late. The realization stunned her. *I'll never forget Quinn. Not even if I return to Seattle tomorrow and never see him again, I'll never forget him.*

The following morning, Dr. Anders pronounced Becky well enough to hobble around her house with her cane. Immensely grateful to Victoria, but aware that she'd kept the younger woman away from her life for two weeks, Becky insisted that Victoria return to her apartment and her own commitments.

Carrying her suitcase, Quinn waited while she hugged Becky goodbye, then followed Victoria down the sidewalk to her car where it took him only seconds to stow the bag in the back seat. He glanced over the car roof at Becky, beaming at them from the porch.

"Becky's watching us."

Victoria's gaze flicked to the porch and back.

Quinn fought the urge to take her in his arms. "Drive carefully."

His voice was gravelly, his eyes dark with emotion.

"I will." Victoria went up on her toes and kissed his cheek. "Thank you, Quinn."

"What for?" he asked gruffly.

"For the best two weeks I can ever remember."

He didn't answer, but he tucked her hair behind her ear, his fingers lingering against her cheek. A muscle twitched along his jawline, his features set in hard lines. Then he stepped back, pulling open the driver's door.

Victoria had no choice. She slid beneath the wheel, he closed the door and stepped back. She turned the key, the engine purred to life, and she shifted into gear and slowly accelerated, waving goodbye to Becky as she pulled away from the house.

All the way down the driveway, she paid scant attention to the road. Instead, she watched Quinn's unmoving figure until she turned onto the gravel main road and the rearview mirror reflected only the empty road behind her.

"Damn," she muttered. "Damn, damn, damn. Why couldn't he have said something? Anything. Like, when I'll see him again."

As she drove into Colson, Victoria grew even more frustrated. The slower rhythm of the small Western town and the people she'd come to know had changed her view of life.

Do I really want to go back to twelve-hour workdays, seven days a week, with no time for friends?

In retrospect, the life she'd lived in Seattle

seemed sterile, without color. Removing herself from her rigid, restrictive routine had forced her to look around. In the years since she'd left college and begun her career, she'd somehow forgotten how much she enjoyed getting to know people. Now that she'd been reminded of the richness of life, she was no longer convinced that becoming a partner in a law firm was worth the cost. Especially after the unforgettable moments she'd spent alone with Quinn.

But I love the challenge of practising law, she reflected. So where does that leave me?

She could apply for a position in a smaller law firm with a lighter workload, she thought, and perhaps change the focus of her practice to general instead of specialized.

Or I could open an office in Colson.

The idea had been lurking in her subconscious for days. Still, consciously acknowledging the thought was startling.

Where did that come from? I can't stay in Colson—my life is in Seattle.

But the possibility was enticing. She'd never seriously considered that she may be able to have a career, a husband and a family. She'd decided early in law school that she must choose between career and a husband. There were too many object lessons in the ruined personal lives of successful attorneys she'd met, both men and women, for her to ignore.

You're building castles in the air, Victoria, she told herself. Even if you don't return to Seattle, there's no guarantee that your future holds a husband and babies.

Because she knew without doubt that a husband meant Quinn. And he'd given no indication that marriage was in their future. Quite the opposite, in fact, for he grimly denied any possibility that he would ever become a husband and father.

Still, that didn't mean that she couldn't remain in Colson and build a different life for herself than the one that waited for her in Seattle.

The possibility of a richer life was tempting. The only part of the equation that remained a question mark was Quinn.

Quinn did Becky's evening chores, shared dinner with her and was home before eight o'clock. Cully looked up from the television and stared at him in surprise when he stalked into the living room.

"What are you doing here?"

"I live here." Quinn dropped into his leather recliner and flipped up the footrest, crossing his booted feet at the ankle.

"I know you *live* here," Cully said patiently. "But you haven't *been* here too often since Victoria moved in with Becky. Why aren't you over there?''

"I was over there. I had dinner with Becky and came home.''

"You had dinner with Becky? What about Victoria?''

"She went back to Colson. Doc okayed a cane for Becky and she sent Victoria home.''

"Ah. I see.'' Cully was silent for a moment. "So, why aren't you in Colson at Victoria's place?''

"Because I'm not,'' Quinn growled, staring morosely at the flickering television.

Cully lifted the remote control, pointed it at the TV and muted the sound. Quinn glared at him.

"What did you do that for?''

"It was too loud. I couldn't hear you telling me why the hell you're here moping in front of the TV instead of at Victoria's.''

"I'm not moping.''

"Yeah, right.'' Cully's tone was patently disbelieving. "If you're not moping, then what the hell is wrong with you? You look like somebody died.''

Quinn didn't answer.

Cully leaned forward in his chair, his gaze searching his brother's face. "I'm serious, Quinn. You don't look too good. What happened with Victoria?''

"Nothing happened. I'm not going to see her again."

"What? Why not?"

"Why not? Come on, Cully. You know why not. A woman like Victoria deserves a better man than me. She needs a husband, and kids..." Struck with the swift mental image of a little boy with Victoria's smile and blond hair, his voice trailed off.

"So? Marry her."

Cully's words jolted Quinn from distracting thoughts of Victoria and blue-eyed babies.

"Bowdries don't have marriages," Quinn said flatly. "They have war zones. I...care too much about Victoria to ruin her life."

"Damn it, Quinn." Exasperated, Cully pushed out of his chair and paced. "Listen to yourself—you 'care' about Victoria? I hate to be the one that breaks the news to you, but you're stone-cold, climbing-the-walls nuts about the woman. You may not be willing to admit it, but that doesn't mean it's not true."

"True or not, how I feel about Victoria doesn't matter." Quinn said. "She has a life in Seattle, a life that's important to her, with a career she's spent years building. What could I give her to replace that? Tell me, Cully, what would she do in Colson? She'd be bored out of her skull if she had to spend a long winter with me on this ranch.''

"Maybe. Maybe not.'' Cully shrugged. "But none of that matters in the long run. Face it, Quinn. You're going to have to marry her or you'll regret it for the rest of your life.''

Quinn opened his mouth to argue with Cully, but his brother's next words stunned him into silence.

"Just like Dad did.'' Cully's stance dared his older brother to argue, but Quinn only stared at him. "You know it's true, Quinn.'' Cully said quietly. "Dad's life with Eileen was bitter and unhappy—for both of them. Dad never got over our mother disappearing without a word; he kept detectives looking for her until the day he died. I think it broke his heart to lose her, and that's why his marriage with Eileen was so bad. He couldn't forget our mother, and Eileen couldn't forgive him for it.''

The silence stretched between them.

"You know I'm right, Quinn. If we really are like our father, and God knows I've heard Eileen say it often enough, then you'd better try to make it work with Victoria, because you'll never be able to let her go.''

Quinn released the footrest and sat forward in the chair. He scrubbed his hand wearily across his eyes and down his face.

"Hell." He propped his elbows on his knees, his hands clasped between, and stared at the floor. He'd already come to suspect that part of what Cully said was true—he wasn't going to easily get over Victoria. The feeling had been growing steadily stronger for days until he was convinced that letting her go would be the hardest thing he'd ever done. For the first time, he allowed himself to consider the possibility that he could have Victoria forever.

And he realized that the reason he'd denied the possibility so strongly was that he wanted it so badly.

"I never thought about marriage, and I don't know a thing about kids, Cully." Quinn waved his hand at the room. "I guess I assumed I'd live my life here without it."

"How does Victoria feel about marriage?"

"I don't know. We haven't talked about it."

Cully dragged in a deep breath, blowing it out in a huff of disgust. "Why not? Becky and I made sure you had plenty of time together."

Quinn's gaze sharpened over his brother's irritated features. "What do you mean you made sure we had plenty of time together?" For the first time, he realized how odd it was that Cully hadn't spent more time with the injured Becky. Nor had there been a stream of women friends visiting her.

"Explain yourself. What did you and Becky do? Did she plan this on purpose?"

"No." Cully shook his head in swift denial. "And even if she had, I wouldn't have let Becky hurt herself just so she could play matchmaker. But once she had Victoria in the house, she didn't waste the opportunity. She ordered me to stay away and made excuses to her friends that visitors were too tiring for her."

Quinn's brows shot up. "And they bought that?"

Cully grinned. "Yeah. Can you believe it? They've got to know that Becky has the stamina of a horse."

"They probably didn't believe her. I'll bet the telephone wires are buzzing with wild stories."

"Nope, Becky convinced the Doc to tell Flora Anderson that Becky had to have absolute bed rest and quiet."

"Well, I'll be damned." A quick grin curved Quinn's mouth. "I wonder how she talked Doc into that?"

"I don't know, but I suspect it had something to do with a winter's supply of her strawberry jam."

Quinn chuckled. "She's a pistol, isn't she?"

"Yup, that's our Becky." Cully pushed away from the heavy console television he leaned against and returned to his chair. "So," he asked, offhandedly. "What are you going to do about Victoria?"

"I don't know." Quinn only knew Cully was right. But the possibility of acting on his feelings both exhilarated and scared him.

Victoria mulled over the questions about her future often during the ensuing days. Saturday found her no closer to a solution. Since she didn't work weekends at the pharmacy, she planned to spend part of the day unpacking the few boxes still stacked, unopened, in the corner of her kitchen. Several pictures still leaned patiently against the bedroom wall, waiting for her to purchase wire and nails to hang them.

Dressed in khaki shorts, a midriff-skimming loose tank top in blue cotton and huaraches, she strolled the few blocks between her apartment and downtown Colson. The midmorning sun was warm, heating her scalp and her bare arms, legs and feet. In sharp contrast, the local hardware store was dim and cool, fans high above in the rafters stirring the morning air with lazy efficiency. Victoria slipped her sunglasses from her nose and dangled them from her fingers, narrowing her eyes to adjust to the sudden switch from bright sunlight to dim store interior.

She wandered up and down aisles, finally locating the nails and wire necessary to hang her paintings and family photographs.

Then she puttered slowly on her way to the checkout counter, browsing the aisles. The old wooden floor creaked beneath her feet, the counters and shelves jammed with a fascinating variety of hammers, saws, nails and screws piled in bins that were cheek-to-cheek with kerosene lanterns and leather harness.

Shopping in Colson is certainly different than shopping in downtown Seattle, she reflected. Curiosity had her picking up, studying, then putting back a half-dozen interesting objects before she finally reached the cash register. The hardware store was busy and she waited patiently in line before she paid for her small purchases.

"Thank you—come visit us again."

"I will, thanks so much." Victoria smiled at the brawny man in the smudged apron behind the counter, collected her bag and turned away. Two steps from the counter, she glanced up to find Quinn striding down the aisle toward her. He was dressed in dusty boots and jeans, with the ever-present gray cowboy hat on his head, and his mouth was set in a firm line, his green eyes narrowed.

He didn't look happy to see her.

She was delighted to see him. She decided that

now was as good a time as any to test Becky
Sprackett's theory.

"Good morning." She stopped dead still in the
middle of the aisle, blocking his way.

Quinn didn't have an option. He either had to
shove her aside, ignore her and pointedly walk
around her, or stop and return her greeting.

He stopped.

"Good morning." He eyed her, his tone carefully polite.

"I dropped in for picture wire and nails," she
said sunnily, waggling a small brown paper bag.
"What brings you here?"

Chatting. He realized in disbelief. She's chatting. One swift glance past her shoulder told him
that the dozen or so men loitering near the counter
and the aisles nearby were watching them with
undisguised interest.

Great, just great. If I'm rude to her, she'll be
embarrassed and it'll be all over town in an hour.

"I needed to pick up a part for a generator."
He stepped aside and paused, glancing meaning-
fully behind her before his gaze returned to hers.
"I'll walk you out."

Startled, Victoria blinked at him. One swift
look over her shoulder at the obviously interested
audience waiting for her reply erased her confusion.

"Oh. Right."

She stepped past him and walked down the aisle, pausing at the entrance, her breath hitching as Quinn bent close, his shoulder and arm brushing hers as he reached around her to shove open the door.

Then she stepped through, Quinn followed, and the door swung closed behind them.

Quinn caught her arm and drew her with him off the sidewalk and around the corner of the hardware store into an empty lot. He stopped in the shade of the roof overhang, out of sight of the street, and turned her to face him.

"What were you doing in there? Didn't I tell you that you shouldn't be seen in public with me?"

"Yes, you did."

"Then why did you say hello to me and stop to chat in front of half of Colson."

"I hardly think a dozen men can be called half of Colson," Victoria protested mildly, crossing her arms across her chest. "Besides, I don't agree with you."

"What do you mean you don't agree with me?"

"I mean," she said pointedly, "that I don't agree that I'll be labeled a fallen woman just because I'm seen talking to you."

Quinn bit off a swearword and glared at her. "You're too stubborn for your own good."

Victoria arched a brow in patent disbelief. "Oh, and you're not, I suppose? You're convinced that my being seen with you is the kiss of death to my reputation. I think you're overreacting."

"Hell." Quinn planted his hands on his hips, his brows lowering. He decided to be painfully blunt. "Look, Victoria, all I do with women is have sex. Period. And everybody in this town knows it."

Victoria didn't even flinch; she just frowned back at him. "And you're proud of this?"

"I didn't say I was proud of it. That's just the way it is. If you're seen with me, all of Colson will assume that we're sleeping together whether we are or not. You won't have an ounce of credibility left with the women in this town, not to mention your aunt and cousin. Do you want to have to explain to your uncle why everyone's gossiping about you?"

"I still think you're overreacting," Victoria argued. "I like you, and I refuse to pretend that I don't. Don't you like me?"

"Yes," Quinn said through clenched teeth, keeping a tight rein on his frustrated temper. "I like you. I also want to carry you off to the nearest empty bed and spend the next twelve hours making love to you."

Victoria caught her breath. The heat that blazed from his eyes and his blunt honesty struck her speechless. The mental image of their two bare bodies wrapped together in the isolation and privacy of a bedroom generated a swift yearning that flooded her with heat.

Quinn saw the shock at his blunt words in her expression, followed swiftly by arrested curiosity and the slow stirring of heat. He groaned.

"Damn, how am I supposed to keep my hands off you when you…" He bit off another pithy swearword and swung on his heel.

"Wait!" Impulsively, Victoria caught his shirt-sleeve, halting him in midstride.

He turned to look at her.

"What?" he growled. The touch of her fingers against his forearm burned his skin and he shrugged free, immediately regretting the loss of contact.

She crossed her arms over her chest once more. The movement drew his gaze to the blue T-shirt pulled taut against her breasts and he nearly groaned aloud, again. He stifled the instant leap of his libido, forcing his attention back to her face. She narrowed her eyes at him consideringly.

"It's obvious the solution to this problem is for us to date."

Dumbfounded, Quinn could only gape at her.
"What?"

"I said," she repeated, emphasizing each word, "that it's obvious that we'll just have to date."

"Are you deaf? Didn't you hear a word I said?"

"Of course I heard you. You told me that you never date, which makes our dating the perfect solution, of course."

"Of course," Quinn repeated blankly. He shook his head to clear it. What was he missing here? "Do you mind explaining how you arrived at this idiotic conclusion."

"If the whole town knows that you never take a woman out on a normal date, then it's logical to assume that if we date, all of Colson will realize that it's a complete departure from your usual behavior. Ergo, they won't assume we're sleeping together, which *is* your usual behavior."

Quinn listened to her, wondering if craziness was contagious, because for some insane reason, she was starting to make sense.

"It won't work." He said grimly. "Much as I wish it would."

He turned and walked away from her. Two strides. Three.

"It's too bad you're so afraid of me." Her voice carried clearly.

Her words stopped him in his tracks.

"Because if you weren't afraid of me," she continued, "we could have had a lot of fun."

Victoria held her breath, wondering if he'd respond. He stood perfectly still for one long moment while she stared at his broad back and silently urged him to turn around. Then he slowly turned on his heel and stalked toward her. One glimpse of his furious face and she wondered if she'd gone too far. She had only seconds to wonder before he stopped in front of her.

He towered over her before he bent slowly forward until his nose nearly touched hers, the brim of his hat shadowing her face.

"What did you say?"

The question was no less lethal for the controlled, quiet tone of the words he ground out. Victoria noted the muscle that flexed in his jaw and barely controlled an urge to step back.

"I said," she responded with admirable calm, "that it's too bad that you're afraid of me because if you weren't, we could have fun this summer."

His eyes narrowed, green flames flickering in the depths.

Victoria ignored the inner voice that told her to run. Instead, she managed to stand her ground and meet his hot gaze without flinching. "You know, Quinn," she drawled, "I haven't known any *boys* that were too shy to ask me out since junior high school. I would have guessed that you were far more mature than that, but..." she sighed and shrugged her shoulders. "Clearly, I was wrong."

Quinn's instinct was to toss her over his shoulder and haul her off to the nearest motel where he could show her just exactly how afraid of her he was, but he managed to restrain himself. Barely.

"I'll pick you up at seven," he growled. "Be ready."

Victoria nodded mutely. He glared at her for a split second longer before he turned and stalked away. Victoria's caution disappeared under a surge of elation.

"You can take me to dinner," she said. He didn't respond and kept walking. "And wear something nice, because I'm going to wear a dress. A sexy dress," she called, louder since he was halfway to the sidewalk. "Oh, and don't forget to bring me flowers!"

Quinn kept walking, refusing to answer her. In seconds, he disappeared around the corner of the hardware store.

Victoria stood motionless, staring after him, an irrepressible smile curving her lips.

"It worked! It actually worked!" she murmured to herself before spinning in a circle, laughing. Grass slipped and dust lifted beneath her sandals, reminding her that she was standing in the middle of a lot, laughing alone, in full view of anyone passing by on the street.

* * *

At three minutes before seven that evening, Victoria tucked one last hairpin into the twist of curls on the crown of her head.

"There," she murmured. She turned in front of the full-length mirror on the bathroom door, glancing over her shoulder to check her dress. The halter collar buttoned just below her nape and blond tendrils brushed against the strip of green silk. The dress left her shoulders and back bare to just below her shoulder blades.

Satisfied that no drift of bath powder smudged the back of her dress, she turned to inspect the front. The bodice was snug, the full skirt falling to just above her knees from the nipped-in waist. The dress was blatantly feminine although it exposed less bare skin than the modest one-piece bathing suit tucked into one of the drawers in her dresser.

The sound of knuckles rapping on the front door reverberated through the apartment. Nerves jumping, Victoria pressed a hand to her midriff and drew a deep breath. She cast one last swift glance over her reflection in the mirror and left the bathroom. Pausing before the door to draw another slow breath in a vain attempt to calm the butterflies fluttering anxious wings in her midsection, she turned the knob and pulled the door inward.

Oh, my. She thought, staring helplessly. He's gorgeous.

Her gaze moved compulsively from Quinn's gleaming black hair, over the planes of his face where a frown curved the firm line of his lips downward, to his white shirt, collar unbuttoned, tucked into gray slacks belted with silver buckled black leather, and further to the ever-present black cowboy boots, dust-free and gleaming with polish.

Her dazed gaze swept back up his long frame, pausing when she realized that he was holding a pearl-gray Stetson in one hand and a bouquet of flowers in the other, before she moved on to his face. She was just in time to see his lashes lift and the scowl turn into something else entirely.

He didn't say a word. He stepped across the threshold, kicking the door shut behind him, and wrapped his arms around her waist. His mouth found hers with unerring precision.

Victoria was vaguely aware of the cool crush of petals and the warm brush of his fingers against her bare back above her dress. The design of the bodice didn't allow for wearing a bra. The fine cotton of his shirt and the thinly lined silk of her dress were all that separated her sensitive breasts from the warm muscles of his chest. It was almost like being naked, skin against skin. But not close enough. Not nearly enough. Locked against him, breast to thigh, his mouth seducing hers with hot intensity, the tiny part of her brain that still functioned demanded that she find a way to get closer. Victoria threaded her fingers into the thick black silk of his hair, her arms tightening around his neck.

Quinn groaned against her mouth, his whole body clenching with the need to pick her up and find the nearest flat surface to lay her down on. Instead, he held on to sanity by his fingertips and reluctantly broke the kiss, tucking her face against his throat while he struggled to catch his breath. Her breasts rose and fell quickly against his chest as she, too, fought to breathe normally.

He smoothed the back of his fingers across bare skin and realized that he was still holding the flowers. He also realized that if she was wearing anything under that flimsy excuse for a dress, it damn sure wasn't much.

He eased her away from him and frowned at her.

"Are you wearing anything under that dress?" he demanded.

Victoria, still trying to marshal her senses, glanced up at him through her lashes, gauging his reaction. "Not much," she admitted.

His eyes went hot.

"Great. Just great," he muttered. "As if I didn't have enough trouble." His arms seemed to have a will of their own and he had to force his reluctant muscles to release her and step back. "Here." He held out the sheaf of flowers, wrapped in a cone of green florist's paper.

"Thank you, Quinn. They're lovely."

She cradled the blooms in her arms, bending to breathe in the scent of roses tucked into the spray of baby's breath and lilacs. She lifted her face and smiled with such pleasure that he felt absurdly pleased that she approved of his choice.

Outside, a car backfired. The sound broke the spell that held Quinn, reminding him that they were alone in her apartment. He glanced at his watch.

"Damn," he growled, noting the minutes that had passed since she'd opened her door and he'd been hit with an overpowering wave of lust too strong to deny. He looked at her. She was smiling mistily at him and he wanted to kiss her again so badly that it hurt to tell himself no. He tore his gaze away from her mouth, tracing the arch of her throat and the strip of skin left bare by the bodice of her dress. The dress wasn't immodest, but the knowledge that only two strips of soft green material separated her bare breasts from his hands damn near made him crazy. And the short, swingy skirt left her legs bare from above her knee to her feet. Even her feet were pretty. Frosted pink nail polish decorated the tips of shapely toes—her bare toes. When he realized he was contemplating erotic fantasies about what he'd like to do with her toes, he yanked his errant thoughts up short.

"Where are your shoes?" he asked testily. "We have to get out of here."

"Why?" Victoria thought he looked like a man pursued by a herd of man-eating crocodiles. "Do we have dinner reservations? Are we late?"

"No, but one of the biggest gossips in town is Elizabeth Price, who just happens to own the only florist shop in town. Which means that half the town knows that I bought flowers this afternoon. Flora Andersen lives across the street and watched me drive up, so by now, the other half of Colson's population knows that my pickup is parked outside your apartment building." He glanced at his watch and frowned again. "I figure we've got another five minutes before Flora gets on the phone and starts telling everyone that I've been here long enough for us to be engaged in serious, down-and-dirty sex."

Victoria's eyes widened, her mouth dropped open. Then she burst out laughing.

"You've only been here ten minutes—maybe fifteen," she said when she could stop laughing. "You must have a *really* wild reputation, Quinn, for anyone to believe that women go from hello to raunchy sex in fifteen minutes."

A slow smile curved his mouth, his green eyes lighting with amusement.

"Oh, honey," he drawled. "Fifteen minutes is more time than I usually need."

The deep drawl sent shivers chasing up Victoria's spine. She lifted a skeptical eyebrow.

"Really? To get started? Or to finish?" she teased.

"Put your shoes on," he growled, unable to suppress the grin that tugged at his lips, sexual tension giving way to amusement. "Before I'm tempted to show you how many hours it would take me to finish."

Chapter Seven

"So, stud," Victoria teased, smiling up at him as they stepped into the Steak House, Colson's one and only supper club. "Ready to face the lions?"

She could feel the tension in the muscles beneath her clasp ease. His facial muscles loosened marginally, a wry smile briefly curving his lips as the remoteness of his green eyes warmed. He shook his head.

"You don't have a defensive bone in your body, do you?"

"Of course I do," she said promptly. "I'm big on defenses. I'm an attorney, remember?"

"Don't remind me," he growled. "I'm trying to forget."

"Well, stop trying. That's not going to change."

He glared at her. She stared back, lifting her chin in cool defiance.

"Good evening. A table for two?"

The hostess's polite question broke their absorption with each other. Quinn's gaze snapped to the young woman. She took a step back, her gaze flicking uncertainly from Quinn to Victoria, then back again and he realized that he was frowning at her. He forced a smile.

"Yes. Please," he added.

"Right this way." The hostess's professional smile held an edge of relief.

Victoria went up on tiptoe, her lips brushing his earlobe.

"Behave yourself, you're terrifying the employees," she whispered.

Before Quinn could respond, she stepped away from him to follow the hostess into the restaurant. Quinn had been so distracted by sparring with Victoria that he'd all but forgotten his qualms about entering the big dining room. He was swiftly reminded as he walked behind Victoria. The pregnant pause in the hum of conversation and the silenced clink of tableware was deafening.

They passed a table of women in their mid-thirties. His gaze registered their widened eyes and raised brows; one brunette nudged her neighbor and pointed. He steeled himself to overhear whispered comments and reminded himself not to lose his temper.

"Quinn."

A hand closed over his forearm, halting him, and he glanced down to see a neighboring rancher. The man was grinning widely.

"Good to see you, Quinn."

"Hello, Angus." His gaze flicked over the rancher's wife and the other middle-aged couple seated at the table. "Evening, Richard." He nodded politely to their wives. The four looked past him, their expressions expectant. Quinn felt Victoria's hand close around his forearm and realized she had stopped beside him.

"I don't believe we know this young lady."

Quinn tensed. His inclination was to pick up Victoria and carry her out of the restaurant, away from his neighbor's curiosity, away from the endless talk and damaging gossip that he was sure would follow.

He glanced down at her. She was smiling with friendly interest at the quartet as if she wasn't concerned about their reaction to seeing her with him.

"This is Victoria Denning—John and Sheila's niece. Victoria, this is Angus McKinstry and his wife, Verna, and Richard Jones and his wife, Marie.''

''Nice to meet you.'' Victoria purposely leaned into Quinn, both hands clasped around his arm at the elbow, her weight resting with easy familiarity against his side. ''It's always a pleasure to meet Quinn's friends.''

She ignored the quick sideways glance Quinn shot her and smiled sunnily at the middle-aged couples. Quinn's stiff introduction told her that he expected the worst, but she saw nothing but warm approval from the four people eyeing her with interest as they returned her greeting.

Behind them, the hostess cleared her throat.

Quinn glanced over his shoulder and slipped his arm from Victoria's clasp, turning her.

''We're keeping the lady waiting, Victoria.'' He nodded to his neighbors, said goodbye and with a hand resting against the small of Victoria's back, steered her after the hostess.

They were stopped once more, by an older, white-haired couple, to exchange friendly greetings before they reached their table.

Both Quinn and Victoria ignored the whispers and raised eyebrows from the table of Eileen's cronies and their husbands just beyond.

Victoria waited until they were seated, accepted menus and the hostess retreated before she spoke.

''Your friends seem like very nice people.''

Quinn looked up from his menu.

"They aren't my friends, they're my neighbors."

"Is there a difference?"

"What do you mean, is there a difference?"

"I thought neighbors in a rural area like Colson became friends through sheer necessity, if nothing else. In Seattle, I'm so busy that I hardly know my neighbors and wouldn't feel comfortable calling on them in an emergency, but I assumed that neighboring ranchers helped each other."

"We do." Quinn gestured at Angus McKinstry. "Angus and his wife have the ranch just south of me. Cully and I help him with branding every year."

Victoria waited expectantly, but he added nothing further.

"And?" she prompted.

"And what?"

"And what else?"

"Nothing else, that's about it."

"What does he help you with?"

"Nothing."

"Nothing? Why not, you help him with branding."

Quinn shrugged. "That's because he needs us. Cully and I don't need his help with anything on our place. We handle what needs to be done."

Victoria was getting a picture of a man so isolated and self-sufficient that it didn't occur to him to ask a neighbor for help.

"But he's your neighbor, like Becky's your neighbor, so you must visit him. His wife probably insists on feeding you dinner every week or so." With three single brothers, all older than she, Victoria was well acquainted with older women's motherly urges to feed their bachelor neighbors.

"No."

"Really?" Victoria considered him over the top of her heavy, gold-tasseled menu. "His wife hasn't shown up on your doorstep with a casserole in one hand and a picture of her unmarried daughter in the other?"

"She doesn't have an unmarried daughter." Quinn eyed her quizzically. "What made you think she did?"

"I just assumed..." Victoria stopped in midsentence, waiting patiently until the waiter had filled their water glasses, taken their order and left them alone again. "What I'm trying to say is that I know what happens when a bachelor lives in the neighborhood—I have three older brothers. They spend half their life eating free food and dodging matchmaking efforts."

"Ah." Quinn's mouth twisted in a sardonic smile. "I don't have that problem."

Not that you're aware of, Victoria realized. She could tell by the conviction in Quinn's voice that he had no idea that the women of Colson considered him one of the town's most eligible bachelors. And what had Lonna said? Oh, yes, Victoria remembered. The most eligible and the least likely to wed.

She propped her elbow on the table, rested her chin on her hand and slowly shook her head at him.

"You're amazing, Bowdrie, absolutely amazing."

"Why is that?" Quinn couldn't help smiling at her. She was the strangest combination of sassy mouth, brains, sharp tongue and mind-numbing sex appeal he'd ever met. And at the moment, she was just plain cute.

"Because you haven't a clue what a catch you are."

"Is that right?" She had no idea how wrong she was, he thought grimly.

"Absolutely. Becky was right."

His gaze sharpened. "Becky? What does Becky have to do with it?"

"She told me that you're a nice guy who's been brainwashed into believing otherwise by that horrid woman who raised you," Victoria said bluntly, not surprised by the swift change in his expression. His green gaze turned cool, his features remote. "And I agree with her."

"You don't know me," he said flatly.

Victoria shrugged, the green silk shifting over bare skin. "Perhaps. But I've seen enough to know that Eileen Bowdrie is wrong." She reached out and brushed her fingers over his hair just above his temples. Startled, he stiffened, but didn't pull away. His black hair was rough silk against her fingertips and she reluctantly drew her hand away. "I knew it." She said with satisfaction.

"Knew what?"

"I knew that Eileen was wrong—you don't have horns."

Quinn laughed aloud, a deep-throated chuckle that had the diners at neighboring tables turning to look at him with astonishment. Some of the occupants frowned with disapproval, some smiled with genuine appreciation.

He didn't even notice. His amused gaze was fastened on Victoria.

"Did she tell you I did?"

"Not in so many words—but after listening to her ramble, I assumed she thought you did."

"I'm sure she thought both Cully and I had horns—and a tail and pitchfork—when we were kids and had to live in the same house with her." Quinn relaxed in his chair, unaware of the diners who cast glances his way. "Of course," he said consideringly. "We always suspected that she flew off on her broom whenever there was a full moon."

"Really?" Delighted, Victoria grinned impishly. "Tell me more. I bet you pulled pranks on her."

"Sometimes."

"So," she prompted. "What was it? Superglue on her chair seat? Worms in the garbage disposal?"

"She didn't have a garbage disposal," he said idly, more interested in her question than his response. "How did a nice, studious girl like you find out about that?"

"I told you, I have brothers."

The waiter interrupted Quinn's laughter.

"Do you have any sisters?" he asked, when they were alone again with steaming plates and filled wineglasses.

"No. I'm the only girl—and the youngest of four."

"Well, that explains it."

"Explains what?"

"Why you're so hell-bent on proving you're right. The only girl and the baby of the family— I'll bet they spoiled you rotten and never once told you 'no'."

"Hah. Are you wrong."

"I'll also bet that those older brothers are protective as hell, aren't they?"

"Now that part you've guessed right," Victoria conceded. "In fact, it's closer to the truth to say they're aggressively overprotective."

Quinn's lips quirked upward. He picked up his wineglass, sipped and returned it to the white tablecloth. His assessing gaze never left hers. "That's probably also why you think you're safe with me. No one's ever harmed the woman with three older brothers to protect her."

"It's true that no one I've dated has 'harmed' me," Victoria agreed. "But that doesn't mean that I've never been hurt. I had my heart broken when I was only thirteen."

"Yeah?" A swift surge of protectiveness hit Quinn. "By who?"

"By a sixteen-year-old cowboy." Victoria watched with amusement while Quinn absorbed her words.

"A cowboy? In Seattle?"

"Not in Seattle. In Colson."

"Here?" Quinn leaned forward, his fingers gripping the stem of his wineglass. "Who was he?" he demanded.

Victoria chuckled and leaned closer. "That was years ago, Quinn, it's too late to punch him."

Quinn realized that he was considering just that. "No wonder your brothers were aggressive," he said repressively. "If you were this difficult at fifteen, I'm amazed they didn't just lock you in your room and bar the door. Tell me his name.''

Victoria looked at the determined glint in his eye and the stubborn set of his chin and gave in. ''His name was Chuck Barrows. He was sixteen at the time and as it turned out,'' she added dryly, ''a real jerk. Of course, I didn't think so at the time.''

''I know the Barrows family. And Chuck's always been a jerk. What did he do to you?'' Quinn wasn't sure he wanted to know, but he was sure he needed to hear the whole story.

''In retrospect, not much. Are you sure you want to hear this?'' she asked skeptically.

''Positive. Tell me.''

''Oh, all right,'' she sighed. ''I was visiting Lonna the summer I was thirteen. I wore braces, my body was as straight up and down as a flagpole, and although I've never been shy, I found myself completely tongue-tied around Chuckie. I could hardly say hello without stammering.''

''And Chuckie?''

''Oh, well,'' Victoria laughed, remembering the sixteen-year-old Lothario. ''He didn't stammer, didn't wear braces and I thought he was Prince Charming. As it turned out, so did all the other girls in Colson and Chuckie thought he was God's gift to women.''

''So how did he break your heart?'' Quinn had

already decided that if Chuck Barrows had laid a hand on her, he'd personally track him down and make him pay.

"Lonna and I took turns helping Uncle John at the pharmacy that summer. Chuck started hanging around. Paying attention to me, teasing me." Victoria waved a hand dismissingly. "You were once a sixteen-year-old guy, you know the routine."

"No. I don't." Quinn's voice was tight. "When I was sixteen, thirteen-year-old girls were off-limits."

Victoria's smile warmed. "Ah. But you were a good guy. And Chuckie was clearly *not*. To make a long story short, he caught me in the alley behind the chutes at the rodeo grounds and grabbed me."

Quinn swore under his breath.

"Before I could stop him, he stuck his tongue down my throat..."

"I'll kill him."

His fierce, soft-spoken threat eased the tightness in her chest that always gripped her whenever she thought of that hot August night. "You don't need to," she assured him. "I bit him."

Quinn's mouth dropped open, his eyes widening. "You bit him?"

"It was pure reflex. But he let go of me so fast I almost fell. He yelled as if I'd killed him." Victoria's smile slipped. "I ran all the way home.

The next day I was mopping floors for my uncle at the pharmacy when I overheard him laughing with his friends about how moonstruck I was. At first I was mortified, then I lost my temper and emptied the bucket of dirty water over his head.''

"Good for you."

"Then I went home to my aunt's house and cried my heart out."

"Well, hell."

Victoria tipped her head sideways and eyed him with interest. ''That's exactly what my brother Sam said when my mother told him what happened.''

''He probably wanted to punch the guy for being such an insensitive jerk,'' Quinn growled. He looked away from her warm gaze and picked up his knife and fork. ''So,'' he said, keeping his gaze on the steak, ''how long did it take you to get over Chuckie?''

"I didn't."

Her soft words brought his head up with a snap.

''What do you mean, you didn't?''

''I never forgot the lessons I learned that day, so in a sense, I never got over Chuckie.''

''And what was the lesson?'' Quinn asked cautiously. ''That all men are scum?''

Victoria laughed. ''No—although I have a few women friends who firmly believe in that theory.

No, the first lesson I learned is to be wary of cowboys.''

Quinn wondered briefly if it was really too late to track down Chuckie and make him pay for breaking her heart. "And the second lesson?"

"Ah. The second lesson I learned is that it doesn't matter how good or bad a man looks on the outside, it's what's on the inside that counts."

"Hmm."

"And it doesn't matter what other people say about him," Victoria continued. "It's what he does that matters. A person can't know that unless she observes for herself."

"Yeah?"

He sounded skeptical.

"Yeah," she echoed, mimicking his disbelieving drawl. "Take you, for instance. You keep telling me what a bad guy you are, but everything you do tells me the opposite."

His lashes lowered, green eyes inscrutable.

"There's something I'm doing that tells you I *don't* want to strip you naked on the nearest bed?"

Victoria flushed. Heat flooded her from the tips of her toes to the roots of her hair.

"No. I'm convinced that sex is on your mind. But I'm also convinced that if you were a man with no conscience, you would have tried to maneuver me into that bed days ago."

"If you were another kind of woman, or you were anyone but John and Sheila's niece, I would have skipped maneuvering and hauled you off to bed two days after I met you."

"But a man without conscience wouldn't care what kind of a woman I am," Victoria said simply. Her curiosity piqued, she abandoned any pretense of eating. "And why does it matter whose niece I am?"

Quinn wished he hadn't voiced that comment.

"John and Sheila did me a favor once. I owe them. I can't have an affair with their niece."

Victoria searched her memory but couldn't recall her aunt and uncle, nor Lonna, ever mentioning a favor in connection with Quinn Bowdrie. In fact, she couldn't remember a conversation in which Quinn's name had generated anything other than general comments or casual knowledge from her uncle John nor her aunt Sheila. Yet Quinn inferred that there was something important between them. What could it be?

"What kind of a favor?"

"They helped me with something a year ago." Her blue eyes lit with curiosity and Quinn groaned silently. "I can tell by the look on your face that you won't give up until I explain, but you have to give me your word that you won't repeat what I'm about to tell you."

Victoria promptly raised her hand. "I swear," she said solemnly.

Quinn's lips quirked. "You didn't need to raise your hand, this isn't a courtroom."

She waved her hand dismissively. "Get to the story, Bowdrie."

"It was nearly a year ago, and I'd had dinner late one night at the Grill. Driving home, I almost hit a car that was parked halfway onto the shoulder with the left rear in the traffic lane. To be honest, I stopped to chew out the driver for doing something so dangerous but I found a sobbing woman inside. Her face was bruised, her lip bloody. She'd found out earlier that day that she was pregnant but when she told her lover, he slapped her around. Seems he was married and hadn't told her," Quinn said grimly. "She was just a kid, too scared to tell her folks, and I couldn't convince her to see a doctor. She wasn't making a lot of sense. I finally talked her into letting me take her to your uncle's house because she knew John and Sheila through church. Sheila doctored her bruises and her lip, then I drove her to Missoula to her aunt's house."

"And gave her enough money to have the baby and get back on her feet?" It was an instinctive guess, but Victoria knew by his swift surprise that she'd guessed right.

"How did you know?" he asked. He'd never

told anybody about finding Angie Patterson, let alone about the monetary help he'd given her.

"I didn't, not for sure. But I'm right, aren't I?" she said softly, her gaze searching his face. "This is Angie Patterson you're talking about, isn't it? And when the rumors flew that you were the father of her baby and had paid her to go away, you didn't deny them because the truth would have been worse for her."

"There are always rumors floating around about me." Quinn didn't deny her analysis. "It didn't bother me that there was another one circulating."

Stubborn man. She sipped her wine and watched him over the rim of her glass. A surge of genuine affection caught at her throat. *He keeps insisting that he's no white knight. But he keeps doing the most honorable things.*

Quinn glanced at his watch.

"I thought we'd catch a movie after dinner," he glanced at her plate. "Are you about through?"

"Yes." Victoria ignored her plate with its neglected meal. She'd been far too interested in Quinn to pay attention to eating.

"More wine?" He lifted the carafe but lowered it when she shook her head. He slipped several bills into the waiter's folder and rose to pull out her chair.

Several more couples stopped them to say good evening as they wound their way through the tables toward the exit. Each time, Quinn introduced her and each time, Victoria was struck with the pleased approval she read on their faces. Although Eileen was aggressive about her dislike of him, some of Quinn's neighbors were clearly glad to have an opportunity to demonstrate their pleasure to see him among them.

Theatergoers' reactions were repeats of the diners at the restaurant, mouths dropped open, heads turned, people stared. Again, warm grins and nods of approval were evenly mixed with frowns and disparaging glances that quickly followed.

Ticket stubs in one hand, his other resting at the small of Victoria's back, Quinn stood in line behind her as they waited for the usher to open the lobby doors. The top of her head reached his chin. He dropped his head forward slightly, just enough to brush his lips against the silky curls and breathe in the scent of musky, faintly oriental perfume. The urge to slip his arm around her waist and pull her back against him, to fit the sweet curve of her bottom against his hips and bury his face against the seductive curve where her throat met the bare curve of her shoulder was nearly overpowering.

"Hey, Quinn."

He jerked, glancing quickly behind him.

"Henry. And Dorothy. Nice to see you."

"Hello, Quinn." The young couple had their two children with them. The little boy stood next to Henry, solemnly eyeing Quinn while the little girl squirmed in her mother's arms, struggling to get down.

Victoria glanced over her shoulder and her hair brushed the underside of Quinn's chin.

"Hello."

She smiled easily at the parents and winked at the children before she glanced up at Quinn.

"Victoria, this is Henry and Dorothy Atkins. Henry and I are both members of the Stockmans' Association. Folks, this is Victoria Denning."

"Denning—of course." Dorothy's gamine face lit with a wide smile. "You're Lonna's cousin, aren't you?"

"Yes, that's right. Are you a friend of Lonna's?"

"We went to high school together," Dorothy laughed. "Most everyone about the same age in Colson went to high school together." Her gaze darted to Quinn before she met Victoria's once more. "Is that where you met Quinn?" she asked with transparent curiosity.

Quinn stiffened and Victoria glanced up at him. His grim gaze met hers in warning but she smiled, mischief twinkling in her blue eyes before she shifted, turning to face him. She leaned against his chest, her fingers stroking down his cheek before she lay her hand, palm down, against the white shirt right above his pounding heart. Her cheek rested against his chest for one brief moment while she gave him a quick hug. His arms lifted in an automatic reflex, and he returned the gesture.

"Goodness, no," Victoria laughed. "I met Quinn at the Crossroads Bar when he saved me from a lecherous man."

"Really?" Dorothy's eyes widened at Victoria's words, her gaze quickly absorbing the ease with which Victoria nestled against Quinn's chest—and the possessive claiming of Quinn's arm wrapped around her. She exchanged a quick, satisfied glance with her husband. "Now *that's* romantic. Henry, why haven't you ever saved me from a lecher?"

"What's a lecher?" The little girl asked.

"Okay, honey," Henry said dryly. "You get to explain this one."

"Hmm. Thanks."

The line ahead of them started to move. Quinn turned Victoria around and pushed her gently into motion.

"Enjoy the show." She peered around him to call.

Quinn heard Dorothy cheerily return the wish before he handed the tickets to the usher, received the stubs back and hustled Victoria into the dim theater.

"Why did you tell her that I saved you?" He asked as soon as they were seated in the back of the theater.

"Uh-oh. Did I tarnish your wicked reputation with rumor of a good deed?" she teased.

"Hell, no," he said shortly. "But it's not true. Beckman can be a real pain, but he wouldn't have actually harmed you."

"Perhaps not, but I didn't know that, did I? And besides, you saved me from a huge amount of irritation and possible assault charges."

"Assault charges? Nah, he wouldn't have gotten even close to assault."

"Perhaps not," she agreed, her face solemn. "But if he'd grabbed me one more time, it's likely I would have punched him and that's assault."

Quinn stared at her blankly before amusement curved his mouth and lit his eyes.

"Beckman outweighs you by at least eighty pounds," he commented.

"Probably." She nodded and narrowed her eyes consideringly. "But I know karate."

"No kidding."

"Absolutely." She lifted her hands. "These hands are lethal weapons."

He caught one wrist in his hand and held her

hand still while he fitted their palms together. His much bigger hand dwarfed hers.

"Lethal weapons, huh?" he huffed in disbelief. "That's the littlest damn lethal weapon I've ever seen."

"Okay, so maybe I'm exaggerating a little."

"Hmm."

The lights dimmed to full dark and the screen came alive. Instead of releasing her, Quinn laid her hand palm down on his thigh, his own hand trapping hers against his slacks and the hard muscle beneath.

Victoria settled closer, her shoulder tucked against his. "You know," she murmured. "For a man who's so worried about his bad reputation, you certainly have a lot of friends. And all of them seemed genuinely pleased to see you tonight."

He didn't answer. Victoria glanced at his profile, illuminated by the light from the flickering screen.

"Maybe you're wrong about what people think about you, Quinn."

"Maybe." He glanced down at her. "Now be quiet and watch the movie."

Victoria hid a small smile of triumph and obeyed.

It was just before midnight when Quinn walked her to her door.

She fumbled with her key, managing at last to insert it, twist and then push the unlocked door inward. She hesitated before turning to face him.

"I had a lovely time tonight, Quinn."

"I'm glad." Quinn leaned his shoulder against the doorjamb. She'd left a lamp on inside the living room and the soft backlight haloed her, gleaming softly against her hair, illuminating half of her face as she turned to face him and casting mysterious shadows over the other half.

"Was it as bad as you thought it would be?"

He considered her words for a moment, surprised that with the exception of moments when he'd steeled himself to meet hostility and censure, he'd been surprised and somewhat dazed by the number of people who demonstrated genuine friendliness.

"No, it wasn't." He mentally shelved confusion about his neighbors' reaction and focused on Victoria. "It was worse."

Chapter Eight

"Worse?" Startled, she searched his face. How could he have missed the outpouring of acceptance from the people they'd met. "But... why?"

"Because it's tough spending time with you and knowing that the evening's going to end with a cold shower."

"Oh."

"Yeah. Oh," he repeated softly. He trailed the backs of his fingers down the curve of her cheek to her throat, pausing to toy with the narrow band of green silk. He pushed away from the door frame, cupped her bare shoulders in his palms and tugged her forward. "Come here."

Victoria went willingly. She, too, had waited for this moment all night. Although she'd purposely treated him with familiarity to demonstrate to anyone watching that Quinn was a man she was comfortable with, she'd found it to be a double-edged sword. Holding his arm, spontaneous hugs, all had fanned the embers of the fire lit when he kissed her hello early in the evening. The need to have him hold her had smoldered all evening.

Quinn wrapped his arms around her waist and bent to brush soft, tasting kisses across her cheekbones, temples and her closed eyelids. When he lingered at the corner of her mouth, she murmured in protest, her mouth seeking his. His plan to claim a sweet good-night kiss went up in smoke when her lips parted beneath his.

He'd never had a woman kiss him with such honest need and the lure of being desired with a heat that matched his own was irresistible. The kiss went from gentle and warm to nuclear meltdown in one hot second. He cradled her head in one hand and held her locked against him while his mouth ravaged hers with fierce need. His fingers moved over her back, found the dress zipper and yanked it down. It jammed and he growled with frustration, caught the edge of silk to rip it aside and froze.

"Hell." He tore his mouth from hers and pressed her face against his throat, his chest rising and falling as he struggled to draw breath.

"Quinn?"

Her voice was thready, husky with passion.

"Sorry, honey." He drew one last deep breath and set her away from him, steadying her as she swayed. "I have to leave. I'm sure Flora stayed up to watch the late show just to make sure she could keep track of what time I brought you home and whether I spent the night."

"Hmm." His words were as effective as a dash of water. Victoria's knees lost their tendency to dissolve beneath her but she didn't take her hands from his forearms. "Well." She drew a steadying breath and eyed him. "If Flora has her stopwatch running, then you'd better go. I don't want to be responsible for ruining the lovely start you made this evening on the new Quinn."

"What new Quinn?"

"Quinn the Gentleman. The Quinn who, I'm sure, knows that proper etiquette requires that he call me tomorrow to tell me again how much he enjoyed our evening together."

Quinn chuckled, the low, amused laugh sending rivulets of warmth through Victoria's already heated bloodstream.

"Pushy, counselor, very pushy."

"Mmm. Perhaps, but if you're really going to

prove that you're not afraid of me, you'll have to date me more than once.''

"You learned a lot about men from those brothers of yours, didn't you? Did they always rise to the bait and do what you wanted when you dared them?''

"Usually." She smiled sunnily up at him. "You figured that out, did you?''

"After I cooled down," he admitted.

"But you still showed up tonight. You could have canceled.''

"Honey, if I didn't really want to be here, I wouldn't have been.''

The lazy drawl and the slow sweep of his heavy-lidded gaze to her mouth and back to meet hers shortened Victoria's breath.

"Oh." It was all she could manage to say.

He brushed a tendril from her cheek, tucking it behind her ear, his fingers lingering against her face. His eyes lost all trace of amusement. He bent and kissed her. Slow and sure, his mouth moved against hers for one long moment before he released her.

"I'll call.''

He stepped back, turned and loped down the steps, disappearing through the exit below.

Victoria stared after him, disoriented. He'd kissed her with passion earlier, but this last kiss was possessive. She felt marked by him, claimed in some indefinable way.

Shaken, she entered her apartment.

Quinn called the next evening. On Wednesday he arrived at the pharmacy just before noon and carried her off to the cafe to share lunch. Both of them ignored the sudden silence followed by the hushed buzz of voices that greeted their appearance. Quinn still tensed, but Victoria quickly teased him into easy laughter. She continued to instruct him in the proper actions required of a male while dating until he threatened to drag her off to the nearest motel if she didn't cease.

Privately, Quinn decided that Colson's approval of his dating Victoria had less to do with their change of opinion of him, and far more to do with the fact that Victoria charmed everyone who met her. She genuinely liked people and her warmth eased the most curmudgeonly of citizens into grudging smiles. Taking cold showers wasn't such a high price to pay for the pleasure of her company.

Victoria devoted several hours on Tuesdays and Thursdays to working in Hank Foslund's office. Because of the time she'd stayed with Becky, clearing the cabinets filled with active files took longer than she'd planned. But when she'd finished with the ones in the outer office, she found that a small stack of misfiled papers atop the cabinet remained, all of them with names scribbled across the top in Hank's decisive scrawl.

She flipped through documents, scanning the names. Clearly, Hank must have another filing cabinet somewhere.

"Maybe in his office," she murmured.

The faint aroma of Hank's pipe greeted her when she pushed open the door to the inner office. A large cherry wood desk sat against the far wall, a high-backed leather chair behind, four client chairs grouped in front. Glass-fronted bookcases held leather-covered law books, a leather sofa stood in front of a draped window, and tucked into a far corner was an old-fashioned, four-drawer, tall wooden filing cabinet.

"Ah-hah."

Victoria flicked on the overhead light and crossed the room. One swift glance told her that the drawers were labeled alphabetically. She pulled open the top one and ran her finger over the file tabs. The file marked Bowdrie was the last one in the drawer. She tugged it free, hesitated when she saw the word Confidential stamped in red lettering across the outside, shrugged and flipped it open atop the drawer.

The uppermost document was a report made four months ago by a detective agency. Curious, Victoria read the narrative describing the efforts made by the agency to locate a woman named Kathleen Constance Parrish.

She glanced at the letter to be filed. Signed by a vice president of a Helena bank, it confirmed the status of a trust fund for beneficiary Kathleen Parrish and inquired if Mr. Foslund's client wished to have any changes made in the second quarter.

Who in the world is Kathleen Parrish? And why is Hank looking for her?

Victoria thumbed through the pages to the bottom of the file, her eyes widening as she read the letter.

"Kathleen Parrish is Quinn's mother."

Quinn had never mentioned his mother's name, but it was clear that he'd been right about his father. Charlie Bowdrie had searched for Kathleen Parrish for years and had continued to do so until the day he died. It also appeared that he'd established a trust fund for her, a fund that now held a substantial sum of money.

Victoria wondered if Quinn knew to what lengths his father had gone to find he and Cully's mother. The fact that Hank kept this particular file separate from the other Bowdrie files led Victoria to believe that perhaps the trust fund was an unfinished matter between the attorney and Charlie Bowdrie.

She filed away the documents and slipped the folder back into place.

She badly wanted to talk to Quinn about the files but knew that was impossible until she cleared it with Hank. She was a bit apprehensive about how Quinn would react to her having access to this highly personal information about his family. He was a deeply private person, and she couldn't help but be concerned that he might resent her intrusion into his personal affairs. Distracted by the contents of the Bowdrie files, Victoria found it impossible to concentrate. A half hour later, she gave up in disgust and left the office.

The air-conditioned office hadn't prepared her for the eighty-degree heat outside. Slipping her sunglasses on the bridge of her nose, she stopped at the cafe for a bottle of ice-cold soda before heading for home. The awnings of businesses along Main Street shielded her from the burning rays of the sun and when commercial blocks gave way to green lawns along Colson's wide residential streets, tall elder trees provided shade. Still, by the time she reached her driveway, she was sweltering, her sleeveless white tank top clinging to damp skin, her upper lip beaded with moisture.

Shrieks and giggles from Cora's shady backyard drew her attention and she veered across the lawn, slipping through an opening in the hedge and into Cora's yard. Following the sounds of laughter, she skirted the sideyard's flower garden and walked around the corner of the big old house, smiling at the scene before her.

Nikki was stretched out in a lounge chair, a straw hat and sunglasses shading her face, her generous curves covered by a brief two-piece yellow bathing suit, long legs tan and bare. Archibald, the cat, was stretched out on the grass beneath the lounger's shade. Angelica skipped in and out of the shower arcing from a whirling garden sprinkler, her green bathing suit and black hair gleaming wetly.

Victoria circled the sprinkler and dropped onto the empty lounge chair next to Nikki.

"Too warm for you?" Nikki asked.

"Too warm to do anything but lie in the shade," Victoria confirmed. She glanced at Nikki. "I thought you worked on Tuesdays."

"I usually do. I swapped a shift with another waitress, she has a dental appointment on Friday."

"Ah. Well, you got the best of the deal."

Nikki laughed. "I couldn't agree more." She sipped from her glass. "How are things going with Quinn?"

"We're dating." Victoria grinned at Nikki's raised brows. "That's all."

Nikki shook her head. "For now," she predicted. "I tried to get information out of Cully about you and Quinn when he was in the Grill yesterday. The most he would say was that he thinks it's about time his brother had a woman."

"Had a woman?" Victoria repeated. "How did he mean that, exactly?"

Nikki grinned. "He didn't elaborate."

"Hmm. Speaking of Cully, how are things going with you two?"

Nikki's animated face fell, her mouth curving downward. "Not well. Most of the time he treats me like his little sister. The rest of the time, I'm not sure he's aware that I'm alive, let alone female."

A wealth of hurt lay beneath her words. Sensitized by her feelings for Quinn, Victoria felt an instant stab of empathy.

"I'm sure you're wrong, Nikki. Besides," she said consolingly, "you said yourself that he treats you differently from other women."

"Yes, like a friend." Her fingers gripped her glass.

"But that's not a bad thing."

Nikki shot her a disbelieving stare. "It's not a good thing when I want to be more than a friend."

Victoria didn't have an answer. If this were Quinn and herself they were discussing, she knew that she'd feel the same way.

*   *   *

The following afternoon was every bit as hot as Tuesday. After a morning at the pharmacy, she changed into her coolest cropped T-shirt, sandals and a short, swingy skirt, and drove to Becky's for lunch. It was after two o'clock when she left Becky's with instructions to stop at the Bowdrie ranch on the way back to town and drop off a pan of cinnamon rolls from the older woman's kitchen.

Victoria was happy to run the errand for Becky since it gave her an excuse to see Quinn. She turned off the gravel road and onto the Bowdrie ranch lane. Well-graded, the lane wound around the bulk of a butte. On the far side of the butte stretched a valley and tucked in the curve of hills lay the ranch headquarters. The road ended in a large open space with the barns and outbuildings on one side and a large, two-story white house on the other.

Victoria parked her car in front of the house and got out, balancing the pan of rolls as she closed the car door. A deep porch wrapped around two sides of the house and three oak rockers sat just to the left of the shallow steps. Tall maples stood sentinel on the grassy lawn surrounding the house, their branches throwing shade across the side porch. Charmed, Victoria's gaze scanned the well-kept old house, guessing that it probably had been built in the early 1900s.

"Hi, Victoria."

Startled, Victoria's gaze flew to the entry just as Cully let the screen slap shut behind him and strolled down the walk toward her.

"Cully—hello."

"What brings you out here? Not that I'm complaining, mind you," he added with a grin. "But Quinn didn't mention that he was expecting you."

"He's not." Victoria lifted the pan. "I had lunch with Becky, and she asked me to drop off cinnamon rolls on my way back to town."

Cully's eyes lit. "Cinnamon rolls. Bless Becky." He took the pan from her and sniffed appreciatively.

Victoria glanced behind him, but the doorway and porch were empty. "Is Quinn around?"

"Yeah, somewhere. We were both in the machine shop a few minutes ago. When I left, he said he was going to check on a mare that's due to foal soon before he came up to the house." He quirked an eyebrow at her and smiled slowly. "Why don't you go find him? If he's not at the barn already, he will be soon. You can give the mare some hay and keep her company while you're waiting."

She glanced over her shoulder at the big barn, flanked by a cluster of outbuildings. "All right, I will. Thanks."

"No problem. I'm starting on the rolls before

Quinn finds out they're here.'' Cully grinned and turned to retrace his steps back to the house.

"Becky said to be sure to tell you two that you have to share,'' Victoria called after him as he loped up the steps.

"Yeah, yeah, right.'' He flashed a grin over his shoulder and disappeared into the house.

The wide lot between the house and barn was powdery black dirt, accented with an occasional clump of straggly grass, and little dust clouds puffed up from beneath her sandals. Victoria reached the barn and paused to peer through the poles. A black gelding stood on the far side of the corral in the shade cast by the barn, head hanging, eyes closed, his tail swishing slowly in the heat.

He didn't prick his ears or look up when she called. Victoria shrugged and walked on to the barn. The big sliding door was closed and she unlatched and shoved it open. It moved easily on well-oiled rollers, the dim coolness beyond the threshold beckoning her inside.

Dust motes danced in the shaft of light through the door and the air was redolent with the scent of hay and animals. The wide alley that bisected the barn stretched ahead of her. Halfway down the aisle, a horse poked its nose over the top of a stall door, nickering softly in friendly greeting.

Charmed, Victoria walked down the aisle toward her. The horse's ears pricked forward, her velvety brown eyes bright with interest and intelligence.

"Hello, you pretty thing," Victoria crooned, holding out her palm. Warm, hay-scented breath huffed across the sensitive skin of her palm, followed by the soft nudge of her nose. Victoria laughed and rubbed her hand over the bristle-dotted, velvety skin of the mare's muzzle. The horse was well cared for, her glossy black hide heavily rounded in late pregnancy.

"Hmm. Cully said I could feed you hay. Maybe I can find you a snack, does that sound like a good idea?"

The horse bumped her again, nickering in agreement.

Victoria looked up and down the aisle, but no bale of hay sat on the clean concrete floor, no bag of grain in sight. Several feet away, however, a wooden ladder was nailed to a thick support post, leading to a square opening in the loft above.

Victoria cautiously climbed the ladder, hand over hand, the smooth soles of her sandals slipping on the worn rungs, until she reached the opening. The loft of the big barn was three-fourths empty. In the far corner, hay bales were stacked against the wall and a bale lay on the floor in front of the stack, the wires clipped, the bale falling apart in sections.

She climbed carefully over the edge of the

opening into the loft, halting halfway across the wooden plank floor to sneeze.

"Oh, great," she muttered, wiping her eyes between sneezes. "Apparently I can add hay to my long list of allergies."

She hurriedly grabbed a ten-inch flake of hay and tossed it down to the main floor, moving quickly but carefully down the ladder.

"Horse," she said, picking up the hay. "I hope you appreciate this."

The mare shifted her feet impatiently, tail swishing in anticipation as Victoria approached. She stopped outside the stall and eyed the gate, the latch, the size of the horse and the distance to the manger at the far end.

She decided not to open the gate and enter the stall with the heavy horse. The adjoining stall was empty, however, and she pulled open the gate, entered and climbed the dividing boards, balancing the hay under one arm. The mare swung around and followed her.

"Hey, none of that," Victoria said sternly as the horse lipped at the hay. Balanced precariously, she reached over the top board of the divider and started to pull the flake of hay into smaller sections.

The mare grew impatient with waiting. She stretched out her neck, opened her mouth, fastened strong teeth in one end of the hay and tugged.

"Stop that." Victoria tugged back.

The mare was stronger. She tossed her head and the flake of hay fell apart, showering Victoria with alfalfa.

Victoria lost her balance and tumbled backward, landing in the deep straw bedding that covered the floor of the empty stall.

Stunned, she lay on her back for a moment, looking up at the rough board ceiling, before she pushed up on her elbows. The mare eyed her with a guileless expression, contentedly munching, green hay trailing from each side of her mouth.

"You..." Victoria's shock quickly turned to laughter.

"What are you doing on the floor?"

Her heart jumped. Her gaze flew to the open stall door. Quinn stood in the opening, frowning at her. Then she sneezed. Twice.

"Are you hurt?" Concerned, he entered the stall and dropped to his heels beside her.

"No," she reassured him, sitting up and dusting her hands together. Her red skirt was rucked up to midthigh, the neck of her white crop-top shoved off one shoulder. Bits of green alfalfa clung to her clothes and skin. Her nose itched; her eyes began to tear and she blinked to clear the dampness.

Quinn's gaze ran over her, lingering on the length of bare legs.

"How did you wind up sitting in the straw, covered with hay?"

"She did it." Victoria waved a hand at the mare. "It's all her fault."

"Yeah?" Quinn looked at the calm mare, then back at Victoria. "Just what did she do, exactly?" He asked mildly.

"I tried to put some hay in her manger and she grabbed it out of my hand. It broke apart and I was sprayed with alfalfa. Then I lost my balance and fell off the divider."

"Maybe you shouldn't argue with a pregnant female several times your size," Quinn suggested.

His solemn tone was belied by the laughter in his eyes. Victoria eyed him for a moment.

"So you think this is funny, do you?" she asked mildly.

He grinned. Lit with humor, his face was stunningly handsome and as always, her heart jolted before it stuttered into rhythm again.

"Honey, if you could see yourself," he drawled, reaching out to pluck a piece of hay from her hair and hold it up for her to see. "You'd probably agree that you're not your usual well-groomed self."

Victoria contemplated swatting his hand away.

Instead, she grabbed fistfuls of the straw and tossed them at him.

He wasn't expecting to be pelted. For a moment, he was perfectly still, yellow straw catching and clinging to his hat, shirt and jeans.

Uh-oh. Too late, Victoria remembered how he'd retaliated with the water hose. She scrambled to her knees, then her feet, in a flurry of skirts, and ran for the aisle and the open door.

Before she reached the stall door, she was showered with straw.

Her allergies chose that moment to decide enough was enough, and she staggered to a stop, caught by a fit of sneezing and coughing. Both exacerbated her tearing eyes and her vision wavered, further disorienting her.

"Damn, honey. I'm sorry."

Quinn's deep voice reached her just as his arm closed around her shoulders, steadying her.

"Water," she choked out between coughs.

"Water, sure, we can do that." He swept her up in his arms and strode down the alley to the back of the barn. He bent and pushed open a door, kicking it shut after him, and carefully set Victoria down. "Don't move, I'll get you a drink."

Victoria sneezed, fumbling in her skirt pocket for a tissue to dry her eyes. Quinn tucked a glass into her hand, folding her fingers around the cool surface.

"Thank you," she croaked. The cold water soothed her throat, easing the tickle that urged her to cough. Quinn left her to push open a window.

Wood rasped against wood, then fresh air, free of the smell of hay or straw, brushed Victoria's face. She sighed with relief, drank more water and for the first time, registered her surroundings.

She was seated on an iron bed in a small room. The old-fashioned, white-painted bedstead was spread with a quilt, the colors muted to pastel blue and white, and a pillow rested against the head rails. The room was spartan, but homey, with a small bathroom off one end, a bureau and a rocking chair beneath the only window.

Quinn left the window and dropped to his heels in front of her.

"Feeling better?"

She nodded. "Yes, much. Thank you for the water—and the fresh air."

"No problem. I shouldn't have thrown the straw at you," he said gruffly. "I just didn't think about your allergies."

"Don't apologize. To tell you the truth, I didn't think about them, either." She glanced around the room. "Where are we?"

Quinn's gaze flicked over the small room. "The hired hand's room."

"You have a hired hand? Where is he?"

"We don't have one at the moment, but when we do, this is where he stays."

"Oh. I see." She coughed.

"Damn." Quinn cupped her shoulders in his hands, then awkwardly patted her back. He hated this feeling of helplessness. He wanted her well, teasing him, throwing straw at him. She sipped the water and drew a deep breath. He bent his head to study her face. "Are you all right?"

Victoria nodded. He stroked her back, the movements comforting. His green eyes were dark with worry. "I'm fine."

The worry didn't leave his eyes and she cupped his cheek in an instinctive, reassuring gesture. "Really, Quinn, stop worrying. This happens sometimes—and it wasn't your fault."

"I shouldn't have thrown the straw at you," he said again, grimly.

"That isn't what made me sneeze and cough," she said gently. "I knew when I climbed into the hayloft that I was pushing my luck. Much as I love the smell of hay, my allergies don't like it. I would have been okay if I'd dropped the hay into the manger and left the barn, but then the mare shook it all over me and I breathed in the dust. The straw probably wouldn't have started me sneezing if I hadn't already had too much hay."

"But it didn't help."

"No. But I refuse to live my life constantly

thinking about whether or not I'll have an allergy attack.'' She met his gaze, her palm smoothing over his cheek, her voice determined. ''This wasn't your fault, Quinn, and I refuse to let you feel guilty.''

Quinn didn't know how to tell her that guilt was secondary to the suffocating fear he'd felt when she'd struggled to breathe between sneezing and coughing. Seeing her vulnerable had smashed what little remained of his defenses. He'd spent most of his nights for the last few weeks lying awake, struggling to come to terms with the knowledge that he needed her. He wasn't comfortable with needing anyone, the emotion was alien to him and he wasn't sure what to do about it.

He wanted her. He needed her. And he didn't know how to tell her. He didn't know what words to use to make her understand that this wasn't just about wanting her body. He wanted all of her— and that scared the hell out of him.

''Quinn?''

Her voice was uncertain. He realized that he'd been staring at her, frowning.

''Sorry, honey.''

His voice was a husky murmur. Victoria's gaze searched his, trying to read the dark emotion that roiled beneath the worry. His big body was tense, muscles coiled, tension evident in the faint tremor of his hands against her back and waist.

He covered her hand with his, pressing her palm and fingertips against his face before turning his head, his lips finding the hollow of her palm. With his eyes closed, the thick black lashes concealed the intensity of his gaze, making him somehow vulnerable. A wave of emotion swamped Victoria.

Then his lashes lifted and his fierce green gaze met hers. Stunned, she couldn't move. Excitement raced through her veins, heating her blood, loosening her muscles and bones. Without knowing she moved, her body swayed toward him.

His hand left her waist. Without looking away from her, he lifted the water glass and set it on the floor away from him.

"I want you."

Driven beyond control, his words were harsh, blunt.

Victoria didn't stop to reason. This was Quinn. And she loved him.

"Yes."

She breathed the word. Quinn didn't wait for another. His hand closed over her bare knee. He lifted her hand from his cheek and slipped it around his neck before wrapping his arm around her waist.

His head bent, his mouth almost brushing hers.

"Hey, Quinn!"

Cully's voice shattered the silence.

Quinn froze. His lashes lifted, frustration roiling in his green eyes.

"Quinn? Victoria?"

Cully's voice sounded louder, nearer.

"Damn." Quinn pushed away from Victoria and stood, catching her hands in his to lift her from the bed. He didn't want his brother to find them in the bedroom but he'd never done anything more difficult in his life than to stop that kiss. His body screamed in frustration. "Come on, honey."

She stared at him, her eyes disoriented and faintly unfocused.

He tucked her hair behind her ear, his fingers trembling with the effort.

"Let's get out of this room. I don't want Cully to find us in bed."

"Oh." Her gaze sharpened, the faint flush over her cheekbones deepening. "Right."

She tugged her hands from his and stepped around him, pausing when he caught her waist and reached around her to pull open the door. Victoria fought the nearly overwhelming need to sink back against him and instead, walked out of the room. Quinn followed and they reached the pregnant mare's stall just as Cully appeared in the open doorway at the end of the long aisle.

"There you are, Quinn." He paused in the doorway, his broad figure haloed by the sunshine outside.

"What's up?" Quinn managed to ask casually.

"I'm going to Kelso's place. He needs a part welded on his horse trailer. I'll probably stop at the Grill for dinner so don't expect me back until late."

"All right."

Cully lifted a hand in farewell. "Nice to see you, Victoria. Come again."

"Thank you, Cully. I will." Victoria was relieved to hear that her voice appeared normal, the passion that had roared out of control only moments before subdued. But then Quinn's palm smoothed from her shoulder to her waist and her nerves jumped, her body leaning into his with an instinctive yearning.

Cully disappeared. Moments later, an engine started and the sound of truck wheels against gravel faded away.

Victoria's gaze left the sunny doorway and she looked at Quinn. His eyes were heavylidded, watchful.

"He'll be gone for hours. Come up to the house with me. I want you in my own bed."

Chapter Nine

Victoria's response was just as blunt, just as honest.

"All right."

His grip tightened. His head lowered before he visibly caught himself.

"I can't kiss you here," he said roughly. "If I do, we'll never make it inside."

His hand left her waist, sliding down her arm to her wrist before he caught her hand in his and set off down the wide aisle. Victoria hurried to keep up with his long strides as he left the barn and swiftly crossed the wide yard between the

barn and the house. He paused, holding the door
for her to enter, then stepped across the threshold.
Victoria got a swift impression of high-ceilinged
rooms and heavy oak furniture before he drew her
up the stairs.

Quinn pulled Victoria into his bedroom and
wrapped his arms around her, kicking the door
shut behind them. His mouth took hers and he
nearly groaned aloud as she welcomed him ea-
gerly, her soft lips parting.

Victoria speared her fingers into his hair, holding him closer while his mouth fed hotly on hers
and he walked her backward to the bed. Without
taking his mouth from hers, he swung her off her
feet and deposited her atop a blue-and-white quilt,
following her down. His heavy warmth blanketed
her body, crowding close and she arched, pressing
him closer. Quinn muttered against her mouth and
pushed her knees apart, wedging between them
and pulling her solidly against his jeans. Body
against body, she sank into the kiss. Quinn's fingers stopped stroking her thigh beneath the edge
of her skirt and moved with sureness over her hip
and beneath her short top. His fingers brushed the
bottom edge of her white lace bra before cupping
her breast with a sure possession that took her
breath. He brushed his thumb over her nipple beneath the lace and she stiffened, arching against
him in an instinctive plea for more.

He groaned, a shudder shaking his body. Then his hand left her. She murmured in protest, but he caught the hem of her T-shirt and pulled it up, his lips deserting hers as he yanked the shirt over her head.

He reached around her and unhooked her bra, the straps falling down her arms, then it followed the T-shirt to the floor.

Disoriented, Victoria heard his low, reverent curse and watched his intent, heavy-lidded gaze follow the movements of his fingers as he cupped her breast, his thumb smoothing over the rucked pink tip. She shivered and her eyelids, much too difficult to hold open, lowered as she concentrated on the unbearable pleasure. Rivers of sensation flowed through her body, swelling her breasts, pulling the nipples tighter as desire pooled in her belly.

His hands left her body. Bereft, she forced her heavy lashes upward. He was standing, stepping away from her.

"Quinn?" She reached for him.

"Let me get my boots off, baby." The words were thick, almost inaudible.

Reassured, Victoria waited, so drugged with desire that she never thought about sitting half-naked on the bed before him. He sat beside her and tugged off a boot, it hit the floor with a thud. The other quickly followed. He twisted, reaching for her but Victoria stopped him, her hands fisting in blue cotton to tug at his shirt.

"Take it off," she murmured, her pulls uncoupling the top two snaps. Quinn grabbed the edges and ripped it open. Victoria pushed it off his shoulders but was distracted by the wide expanse of his sleek, tanned chest. She abandoned his shirt, flattened her hands over his collarbone, then stroked the washboard muscles of his midriff to his navel and the beginning traces of silky black hair that arrowed downward. Her thumb tested his navel. He growled out an oath and shrugged out of the shirt, reaching for her as she leaned into him, her arms going around his neck to bring them together, silky bare breasts and midriff against the satiny skin of his chest.

Their mouths fused hotly together, he tumbled her backward on the bed, one hard thigh between hers. His hand found her knee and stroked upward, the hem of her skirt pooling over his wrist. His fingers brushed the damp silk of her panties and she bucked under his hand.

Quinn was barely capable of thought, let alone speech. He ripped open his jeans, fumbling in his pocket as he foggily remembered that he needed to protect her. She was nearly frantic beneath him. Driven by the need to claim and mate, he ripped the white silk underwear, covered himself and entered her in one fierce rush.

She stilled. He froze, seated deep within her.

Remorse dragged him back from the edge. "Did I hurt you?"

"No." Her voice was slurred, thick with pleasure. "No. Please…"

Relieved, Quinn obeyed the tug of her arms and lowered his mouth to hers. Her hips lifted, urging him on, and instinct took over, driving them both to fulfillment.

Weeks of wanting and waiting to have her dissolved. Quinn held her tightly, their bodies sealed together, his face buried against her throat as his breathing slowly returned to normal. She stirred, shifting beneath him.

"I'm too heavy," he muttered.

"No." Her arms contracted, holding him against her. "Don't go."

"I'm not going far." Her words eased something anxious inside him. He shifted to the side, his face beside hers on the pillow, his arm across her waist, fingers cupping the warm weight of one breast, his thigh lying heavy and possessive between hers.

Her hands made little, stroking movements against his back, her pulse throbbed at the hollow of her throat.

Strands of her hair trailed across the few inches of pillow between them, and he rubbed his cheek against the fragrant softness. His fingers left her breast to smooth the tousled mass back from her temple.

"Mmm."

Eyes drowsy, she smiled tenderly. Quinn couldn't resist tracing the faintly swollen curve of her bottom lip with the pad of his thumb. That led to tasting her. She responded, her mouth warm, slow and loving beneath his.

He trailed his hand down her throat, lingering over the flushed, silky swell of her breasts, the inward curve of satiny midriff. His fingers tested the span from the dainty indentation of her navel to the outer curve of hip before he found the damp curls at the juncture of her thighs. She was swollen and sensitive, and her fingers tightened against his shoulders when he brushed her soft, heated core. She sighed, her mouth parting to the gentle nudge of his and his body tightened when she sucked delicately on his tongue, lazy fires raging to life again.

Reluctantly, his fingers left her, his mouth lifting from hers. He shifted off the bed.

"Quinn? What's wrong? Where are you going?"

"Nowhere, honey," he rasped. "This time, I want us naked," he said as he shoved his jeans and underwear down his legs.

Victoria felt her throat go dry. He was fully aroused, powerful and intimidating.

He bent over her, stripping her skirt and the torn silk undies quickly down her legs. Then he tugged her sandals off and tossed them on the floor with her clothes. Before Victoria could blink, his warm weight blanketed her once again, his face inches above hers.

"Now, where were we?"

"Right here." Victoria lifted her lips to his, sinking back against the pillow when his tongue surged hotly into her mouth.

Filled with passion and the wonder of making love, the afternoon passed too quickly. Neither of them made promises. There was no pillow talk about tomorrow, no declarations of love. Both were reluctant to dispel the sheer magic of their time together by raising the thorny issues that lay unresolved between them. Quinn didn't ask her if she would stay in Montana; Victoria didn't ask him if he could move past his affection-starved childhood and offer her love, marriage and children.

Still, something deep inside told Victoria that Quinn felt more for her than lust. The intensity of his lovemaking, the gentleness of his touch as he tucked her hair behind her ear or traced his fingertips over her face made her feel cherished.

Late that evening, after he'd insisted on following her home and kissed her good-night at her door, she watched from the window as he drove away.

Just because he didn't say the words doesn't mean he doesn't care. I didn't say the words, either, she told herself. But Victoria knew why she hadn't told Quinn she loved him. The knowledge was too new, and she was too unsure of him.

Would Quinn ever be able to say the words to her?

Victoria woke the following morning to another day of clear blue sky and rising temperatures. By the time she reached Hank's law office, it was eight-thirty and the thermometer already read seventy-two degrees.

Simple though the routine of responding to phone calls was, still it was nearly ten-thirty before she turned to the mail. She shuffled through the envelopes, halting abruptly when she recognized the return address of the Los Angeles detective agency from the Bowdrie file.

Frowning, she slipped the metal letter holder beneath the flap and ripped the envelope open, extracting the single sheet of letterhead.

"Oh, my God."

Shocked, Victoria reread the letter.

"After all these years, they have a lead on Kathleen Parrish."

Her first instinct was to telephone Quinn and

share her excitement. But her legal training refused to let her. Instead, she flipped through her wallet and found the phone number for Hank's daughter in Florida.

It took only a few moments to get him on the line and fill him in on the letter's contents.

Hank sounded as stunned as Victoria had felt when she first read the letter.

"They don't know her present whereabouts." She continued. "But a woman by the name of Kathleen Parrish, with a matching birth date, renewed her passport a year ago. She was living in Paris at the time but she's moved around a lot in the last twenty years."

"In Paris? That doesn't sound like Charlie's Kathleen Parrish. She had a high school diploma and worked as a waitress in a local cafe when he met her. Where would she have gotten enough money to travel in Europe?"

"I don't know, but the date of her original passport seems to indicate that she left the States within a year of disappearing from Montana. And Hank," Victoria added. "There's something else—she traveled with an infant, a little girl named Rebecca Parrish."

Hank swore softly. "So Quinn and Cully may have a sister."

"It looks that way." Victoria hesitated. "This

file is marked 'Confidential', Hank, but I'd like your permission to tell Quinn.''

''I'm not sure that's a good idea,'' he said slowly. ''There's no way of knowing whether this lead will turn into another dead end. I'd hate to raise Quinn and Cully's hopes only to have this trail turn cold as so many have in the past.''

''But this is different, Hank. This isn't just a clue to their mother's whereabouts, this is new information. It's likely that they have a sister, one they never knew existed. Don't you think they should be told?''

''I see your point,'' Hank conceded. ''I'll call the travel agency and see how quickly I can catch a flight.''

''No, you don't have to do that,'' Victoria said quickly. ''I can handle it. I'd like to, Hank.'' She hesitated before continuing. ''I've been dating Quinn. I'd really like to be the one to tell him.''

''Doesn't that make this more complicated? Are you sure you can be objective if your personal feelings are involved?'' he asked dubiously.

''Yes, I'm sure I can.''

''All right,'' he said with sudden decision. ''Handle it, Victoria.''

''Thanks, Hank.''

''And Victoria…''

''Yes, Hank?''

"Give some thought to staying in Colson. I've been thinking that I could use a partner."

Stunned, Victoria was speechless.

"Hank, I don't know what to say," she stammered at last. "Are you serious?"

"Absolutely. I'd like to have you in the office permanently," he said bluntly.

"Thank you, Hank. I'll think about it, I really will."

She said goodbye and hung up, staring blankly at the sheet of paper in front of her for a long moment.

A partnership with Hank. Why didn't I think of that? What a wonderful opportunity.

But she could devote little time to Hank's startling proposal. She had more pressing matters. She grabbed the phone and punched in Quinn's telephone number.

"Yeah?"

"Quinn." She breathed a sigh of relief. "I need to talk to you. Are you going to be home for a while?"

"For you honey, always. Come on out."

"Is Cully there?"

"No. He's over at Kelso Nickell's place. Why?" His voice sharpened, the lazy drawl disappearing.

"I'll tell you when I get there."

"All right. Drive carefully."

Victoria drove carefully, but faster than usual. When she pulled her little car up before Quinn's front gate, he exited the house and strode down the sidewalk toward her.

She met him halfway, returning his kiss with appreciation.

Quinn kept his arms wrapped around her waist when he lifted his mouth from hers.

"So what's the rush, sweetheart?" His voice was deeper, huskier than normal. "Why did you want to talk to Cully?"

"Actually, I wanted to talk to both of you. But I can catch Cully later. Can we sit down?"

"Sure." He draped his arm around her shoulder and turned back to the house. "Let's have a seat on the porch out of the sun."

"Great."

Their hips brushed companionably as they climbed the steps. Victoria took a seat in one of the oak rocking chairs, removed the detective agency's letter from her purse and set the leather bag on the floor beside her.

Quinn dropped into a chair and leaned forward, propping his forearms on his thighs, his gaze assessing her solemn features.

"Tell me."

Victoria glanced at the letter in her hand, then

at Quinn. He watched her, quietly curious. She cleared her throat.

"You know that I've been working at Hank's office while he's gone? Taking phone calls, organizing his files, and so on?" Quinn nodded and she continued. "I've also been opening his mail." She glanced down at the letter once more and drew a deep breath. "This came this morning. I think you should read it."

Quinn took the envelope from her hand. He removed the letter.

Shock moved across his features, followed by quick anger, then just as swiftly by stunned shock once again.

"My mother left the country? No wonder Dad couldn't find her," he muttered. "And she had a baby."

His green gaze met Victoria's, his lashes narrowing. "A little girl. I have a sister?"

"It seems likely. The age of the infant on the passport makes it almost certain that your mother was pregnant when she left Montana."

Quinn stared at her for a long moment, his face set in forbidding lines, before he surged out of his chair and stalked to the railing. His back rigid, he stood, staring silently out across the acres to the rise of buttes in the distance.

"The agency doesn't know Kathleen and Rebecca's current whereabouts and the passport renewal information is more than a year old,'' Victoria said. ''Hank was concerned about giving you false hope that your mother and sister may be located anytime soon, but I thought it was important that you know that you may have a sister. Somewhere,'' she added, ''And that the agency will continue to search for your mother.''

''Thanks for telling me.'' His voice was short, tight with anger.

''Quinn…'' Victoria rose and crossed the porch, covering his clenched fist with her own palm and fingers. ''I know this is a shock, but…''

His gaze left the horizon to focus on her. Laserbright and furious, his eyes were filled with anger.

''A shock?'' he said bitterly. ''Yeah, I guess you could say it's a shock to learn that my mother not only deserted us but she took my sister with her. A sister she never bothered telling us about. A daughter she never told my father he had.''

Victoria ached for the pain and betrayal written on his set features.

''I'm sorry, Quinn,'' she said softly. ''Maybe Hank was right, maybe I shouldn't have told you.''

''No.'' He shook his head in quick denial. ''No, I'm glad you told me.'' He turned his hand beneath hers and threaded his fingers through hers. Then he drew her with him and dropped into the rocking chair, pulling her down onto his lap before he wrapped his arms around her.

"None of this is your fault," he said, the words muffled against her throat. "It's Bowdrie history. And like most Bowdrie history, it's not good."

They sat for long moments, Victoria's arms tight around his neck, Quinn's arms wrapped around her waist and shoulders. The ranch drowsed in the hot afternoon sun.

Victoria brushed her lips against his temple and he lifted his head, a subtle tension invading his big body beneath hers.

"Victoria?"

"Let's go upstairs," she murmured, aching to hold him and offer the forgetfulness and comfort of making love.

Fire blazed in his eyes, heat licking swiftly beneath his skin in a flush of red across his cheekbones.

Without another word, he stood, carrying her into the house and up the stairs.

The peaceful quiet of the small apartment was disturbed by knocking on the door. Surprised, Victoria glanced at the clock on the small table next to her.

"Nine forty-five." She murmured. Her heart beat faster. Could it be Quinn? She glanced quickly out the window but the street below was empty, with no sign of Quinn's pickup. Her heart rate returned to normal and she pushed out of the comfortable chair, crossing the room to the door.

"Who's there?" she called, her hand poised on the doorknob.

"It's me, Nikki."

"Nikki?" Victoria unlocked the door and pulled it open. The woman on her doorstep was a paler version of her usual colorful self. A loose black T-shirt was tucked into her jeans, her face pale and scrubbed free of makeup. "Come in." Nikki stepped past her into the living room and Victoria swung the door closed, locking it securely. "What's wrong?"

"I have to leave Colson." Nikki said abruptly, her face strained. "And I'm hoping you can give me some advice about where to go in Seattle."

Stunned, Victoria gestured to the sofa. "Of course. Let's sit down." Belatedly, she remembered her manners. "Would you like some tea?"

"No, thanks." Nikki halted abruptly and dragged her fingers through her hair. "Yes, actually, a cup of hot tea sounds good."

"All right." Victoria changed directions and moved into the kitchen. "This will only take a moment, I made a cup of tea only a half hour ago so the water is still hot." She flicked on the burner under the teakettle and pulled open cabinet doors to take down mugs and tea bags. Nikki leaned against the doorjamb, watching silently. Her thick mane of auburn hair was tousled from the movements of her fingers. Golden freckles dotted the creamy skin over her nose, highlighting her fair skin. Her brown eyes were troubled, faint blue shadows smudging the delicate skin beneath and Victoria suspected that Nikki had been crying. "Why do you have to leave Colson? What happened?"

Tears welled and Nikki brushed them away impatiently. "I just need to get away. This town is suffocating me."

"I see." Victoria guessed that there was far more to the story. Behind her, the teakettle whistled merrily. "Ah, here we go." She switched off the burner and poured boiling water over the tea bags in the mugs. She took spoons from the silverware drawer, collected the sugar bowl, and handed one steaming mug to Nikki. "Let's go into the living room and sit down."

She deposited mug, spoons and sugar on the coffee table and curled up on the sofa, tucking her feet beneath her.

"I can see that you've been crying, Nikki," she said gently. "Won't you tell me what's wrong?"

"I can't talk about it without crying," Nikki said. "And I've cried until my head aches."

"All right," Victoria conceded. "But can you

at least tell me if someone has hurt you? You haven't been assaulted, or…''

"No," Nikki said quickly. "I haven't been hurt physically.'' Tears spilled over and trailed slowly down her cheeks. "Not unless you count a broken heart as 'physical'.''

With her own heart in peril, Victoria was hypersensitive to the pain behind Nikki's words. "Oh, Nikki.''

"Isn't this ridiculous?'' Nikki took a tissue from her jeans pocket, dabbing at her eyes, wet cheeks and nose. "Lonna and I warned you about the Bowdrie brothers. Now I'm the one with a broken heart. How could I have been so stupid as to fall in love with Cully!'' She glanced at Victoria and shook her head miserably. "I'm a complete idiot.''

"No," Victoria said swiftly, leaning forward to clasp Nikki's forearm. "You're not. If Cully Bowdrie doesn't have the good sense to see what a wonderful person you are, then he's a fool.''

"No. I'm the fool.'' Nikki stood quickly. Too agitated to sit still, she paced the floor. "I actually thought he liked me. He always joined us when I went to the Crossroads Bar with friends, danced with me, teased me, talked to me.'' She halted in midstride to look at Victoria. "He doesn't do that with everyone, you know.'' At Victoria's nod, she resumed pacing. "I thought we were friends,

growing closer, that maybe someday… Well,"
she laughed bitterly, choking back tears. "Tonight
I learned exactly what he thinks of me."

"What did he do?"

"I was at work—I had the early afternoon and
dinner shift at the Grill. Cully came in for dinner,
and I joined him for coffee on my break. We were
talking about you seeing Quinn, and he thinks that
you're the perfect woman. You're a college grad-
uate—I have a high school diploma. You have a
high-powered career as an attorney—I'm a waitress at the Crossroads Grill. You're sophisticated—I'm small town. You have an impeccable
reputation—I'm a direct descendant of the owner
of the oldest house of pleasure in Colson." Nikki
ticked off the comparisons, her voice matter-of-
fact.

"But none of those things mean that Cully
doesn't, or couldn't, care for you," Victoria argued. Nikki's brown eyes held a wealth of pain
and sadness.

"Yes, they do." She shook her head. "I saw
his face when he was talking about you and
Quinn, Victoria. I heard his voice." She was silent for a long moment. "I'll miss Aunt Cora and
Angelica desperately, but I have to leave Colson.
I need to find out if I can make a life for myself
away from this town—and away from Cully."

"All right." Convinced that Nikki was determined, Victoria rose and collected pen and paper from a drawer in the small table near the window. "I can see that you've made up your mind to go through with this. And since you have—" she jotted a note on the paper. "—I'm going to send you to my parents' house."

"Oh, I couldn't..." Nikki protested.

"Yes, you can. I insist—you can stay with them until you find a job and become comfortable in Seattle, then, if you want to move into an apartment of your own, fine." She picked up the portable phone from the coffee table and punched in numbers. "Shh." She ignored Nikki's attempt to protest further. "Mom? Hi, sorry to call this late—you weren't asleep, were you? You're reading in bed? Good. Mom, I have a favor to ask..."

Ten minutes later, she said goodbye and broke the connection.

"You're all set," she said with satisfaction. "Mom's delighted to have you." She finished writing directions and tore the sheet from the pad to hand it to Nikki. "You're not leaving tonight, are you?"

"I wanted to," Nikki admitted. "But I need to pack and explain why I'm leaving to Angelica and Aunt Cora. Saying goodbye to them isn't going to be easy."

"No, it won't. Will they understand?"

"Cora will," Nikki nodded with conviction.

"She's always encouraged me to go away to college or a trade school—but there was never enough money. She only has a small pension and we needed my salary to make ends meet." She stared at the sheet of paper for a moment, before adding almost to herself. "I have a bit in savings to tide her over, but I'll need to find a job quickly so I can send her money each month."

"There are hundreds of restaurants in the Seattle area. I know you're an excellent waitress, so if you want to continue in that line, I'm sure you'll have no trouble finding a job. Or are you thinking of something different? What do you want to do?"

The small smile that briefly curved Nikki's lipstick-bare lips was quickly gone, but it gave Victoria hope that the younger woman's naturally sunny spirit would rebound in time.

"You won't laugh if I tell you?"

"Absolutely not."

"I've always wanted to manage a bed-and-breakfast. I love to cook, redecorate, entertain people." Nikki's slender shoulders lifted in a self-deprecating shrug. "Pretty silly, huh? A small hotel manager/chef in Colson."

"I don't think it's silly at all." Victoria waved a hand. "And why not in Colson?"

"We have one motel and only short-order cooks in Colson, not chefs. Anyway." Nikki stood. "It doesn't matter. I'll never have the money to go to school."

Maybe you will, Victoria thought, her mind busily sifting through options.

"I'd better get going. I have a lot to get done if I'm going to leave in the morning."

Victoria rose and followed her to the door. "Call me when you get to Mom's," she told her. "Because I'll worry whether you've made it safely."

"Yes, ma'am." Nikki's smile flashed briefly. "I can't begin to tell you how much your help means to me, Victoria." Her voice broke.

Victoria pulled her into her arms and hugged her tightly before stepping back, her own eyes damp.

"You have no idea what a favor you're doing for me," she joked with a wavery smile. "My parents have suffered from empty-nest syndrome ever since I left the house—I'm the youngest. They'll love fussing over you."

"I hope so. Thank you for this." Nikki clutched the sheet of paper.

"You're welcome. Take care."

Victoria stood in the doorway, lifting a hand in farewell when Nikki paused at the bottom of the stairwell to look back and wave. Victoria closed her apartment door and methodically turned the locks, her mind preoccupied with Nikki.

The phone rang, startling her from her thoughts and she snatched it up from the table, certain that it was her mother calling back with a forgotten detail.

"Mom?"

Her greeting was met with silence.

"You're expecting your mother?"

The deep voice flooded her with relieved delight.

"Quinn!"

Victoria dropped into the armchair, smiling with pleasure.

"Are you expecting a call from your mother?" he asked. "Should I hang up?"

"No," Victoria said quickly. "I was talking to her only a few moments ago. When the phone rang so soon after we'd hung up, I assumed she'd called back to tell me something she'd forgotten earlier. Your voice startled me."

"Yeah? I don't sound like your mother?" His deep voice held amusement.

"No," Victoria said dryly. "Mom's voice is definitely more soprano, while yours is more bass. Now my dad, on the other hand, sounds a bit like you."

"Yeah? Is this a good thing?" Quinn asked warily.

"Absolutely," Victoria said promptly, smiling

at his small hum of appreciation. "Did you spend time with Becky tonight?"

"Yes. She made dinner for us, and I helped her upstairs to her room before I left."

"Was she feeling all right?" Quick concern swept Victoria. "Do you think she should have been standing and using her ankle long enough to make dinner?"

"No, I don't. Which is why I insisted on barbecuing steaks on the grill. She put potatoes in the oven to bake, then cut up a salad while she sat on a lawn chair to keep me company while I watched the steaks," he chuckled. "Then I had to fight with her again to let me wash the dishes while she sat down to dry them."

Victoria laughed. "And I bet she scolded you and told you to go home all the while you were helping her upstairs, didn't she?"

"I see you know our Becky well," he said dryly.

"Not nearly as well as I'd like to," Victoria confessed with a smile in her voice. "She's a lot of fun. If I hang around her long enough, I'll be ready to play poker in Vegas."

"Hah," Quinn snorted. "If you keep playing poker with Becky Sprackett, you won't have any money left to take to Vegas. She cheats, you know," he warned.

"No!" Victoria feigned surprise. "Not that sweet little lady!"

"That sweet little old lady will have you betting your gold fillings—and she'll collect them too, when you lose. Which you will, because she's a card shark."

Victoria giggled. She couldn't remember the last time she'd giggled.

"If I didn't know better, I'd guess that you've never beaten Becky at poker."

Silence reverberated over the line.

"You'd guess right," he admitted, faintly disgruntled. "I came close one time." He added. "But I couldn't prove that she slipped an ace off the bottom of the deck so I had to let her claim the pot."

Victoria could only laugh.

"I'm serious, Victoria," Quinn warned her. "Don't bet money with that woman. She used to wipe out Cully's and my piggy banks on a regular basis."

Quinn continued to relate outrageous stories about Becky. Time flew by as Victoria sat curled in the chair, connected to Quinn by his voice and their shared laughter.

"Are you working at the pharmacy tomorrow?" he asked much later.

"Yes," she responded. "Sheila has a dental appointment in the morning so my being available was good timing. Uncle John wants me to open the store at nine.''

"Then I'd better let you go," he said reluctantly. "Victoria…" His voice was deeper, husky and the brief silence was charged with emotion. "I watched the sun go down alone tonight. It wasn't the same without you here. I missed you."

"Did you?" Victoria's eyes went soft and lambent.

"Yes," he said gruffly.

"I miss you, too." Victoria couldn't erase the yearning that lay beneath her words, her voice an unsteady thread of sound.

"Good. I'd hate to feel this way alone." The words were a husky murmur. "Go to bed, honey. I'll call you tomorrow."

"Goodnight," she whispered.

"Night."

Quinn hung up the telephone and crossed his arms beneath his head, staring up at the darkened ceiling of his bedroom. He wanted her. But the ache went deeper than the physical need that rode him and had him shifting restlessly against the sheets. He wanted her close enough to touch, not just while they were making love, but all the time. That meant having her living in his house and sleeping in his bed.

He had to convince her to stay in Colson. But

how? There were no law offices in the small ranching community that would offer her a career to compare with a partnership in a high-powered Seattle firm. Her work was important to her; he couldn't and wouldn't ask her to give it up.

It's ironic that I'm worried about her opportunity to practice law, he realized. His deeply embedded dislike of attorneys and the law profession had been shaken by Victoria. He still didn't like lawyers, but he had to admit that perhaps not every attorney was a bad seed. Especially not Victoria.

He went over and over the problem but could find no solutions. When he finally fell asleep, his subconscious continued to wrestle with the puzzle with little result.

Quinn took Victoria to dinner the following evening, but kissing her good-night at the door nearly did him in.

"I can't stay," he ground out.

"Why?" Victoria was barely capable of speaking. His mouth was furnace-hot against her throat. Her dress was unbuttoned to the waist and pushed off one shoulder, his hand cupped possessively over the white lace of her bra.

"Because I'm damned if I'll take you and leave you in a few quick minutes," he muttered, his lips brushing the upper swell of her breast above white lace. "And your neighbors would have a field day gossiping about you if I spent the night."

"Mmm." Victoria wanted him so badly that she didn't think she cared what the neighbors said, but she knew that gossip mattered to Quinn. So she didn't resist when he pulled away from her.

"I don't want to leave you," he groaned. He bent and kissed her, his mouth fierce with frustration and hunger. Then he yanked open the door. "I'll call you."

He left. Victoria heard him stride down the steps, heard the thud of the outer door, and waited until the growl of the truck engine faded into silence before she moved.

She twisted the locks closed and drifted into her bedroom, still dazed by the force of the passion that always flared between them. She understood Quinn's sexual frustration all too well for she suffered, too.

And she still hadn't told him she loved him, nor asked him about their future. She hadn't found the right moment. Sighing, she showered and climbed in bed, dreams of Quinn keeping her twisting and turning until dawn.

Unfortunately for Victoria, Quinn was kept busy at the ranch with one emergency after another over the next few days.

After three days of only hearing his voice in after-midnight telephone conversations she was beginning to feel seriously deprived. Then the bells on the shop door jangled shortly after lunch and she glanced up just in time to see Quinn walk into the pharmacy.

"Quinn!" She didn't care that several customers turned to stare. She didn't care that the smile on her face and the pleasure in her voice must surely have spoken volumes about how she felt about him. The only thing she cared about was Quinn.

He was wearing work clothes—faded jeans and dusty boots, with the sleeves of his blue work shirt folded up over sun-browned forearms and the ever-present gray Stetson tilted over his forehead.

His eyes lit when he saw her, a smile curving his hard mouth.

"Afternoon, Victoria."

For once, he didn't seem to care that there were people watching. Victoria halted in front of him and brushed a smudge of dust from his shirt pocket.

"Have you been playing in the dirt again?" she teased.

"If you call chasing thirty-odd cows and calves back through a downed fence, then yes, I guess I've been 'playing' in the dirt," he said dryly.

"Uh-oh. Did you find them all?"

"I think so." He tucked a strand of hair behind her ear, his fingers brushing gently against her cheek and the soft lobe of her ear. "What have you been doing?"

"Working. And missing you," she added softly, lowering her voice so only he could hear.

His eyes darkened.

"Yeah?" he asked, just as softly.

"Yeah," she mimicked, just as quietly.

"Maybe we can do something about that tonight," he murmured. "Wait up for me."

Her heart beat faster. "What time will you be there?"

"I don't know. I'm buried in work. The only reason I'm in town now is to pick up a part for a water pump. But I'm not going another night without seeing you. Do you care how late it is?"

"No." She shook her head, smiling with pleasure.

The door opened behind them, bells jingling, but neither of them noticed the customer enter. But the woman saw them. There was no mistaking their intimacy. Quinn's head was bent toward Victoria, her face turned up to his. The very closeness of their bodies shrieked familiarity.

The sight infuriated Eileen Bowdrie.

"Well, isn't this cozy?"

The acid tones shattered the spell that held the

two lovers. Quinn stiffened, his shoulders squaring as he shifted to face his stepmother, instinctively shielding Victoria.

"Eileen," he acknowledged, his voice impersonal.

Except for one frigid glare, she ignored him, all her attention on Victoria. "It's obvious that you don't listen to good advice, young woman. Your poor aunt and uncle must be worried sick about your liaison with a man as unacceptable as Quinn." Her mouth twisted, pursing in distaste.

"My aunt and uncle respect my judgment," Victoria said pointedly, in an attempt to be polite.

"Humph." Eileen dismissed the words. "Your judgment is clearly impaired if you're expecting anything but an affair with Quinn. He's just like his father. All you'll get from him is misery and heartbreak when he's unfaithful, which he's sure to be. He'll never marry you, you know."

White-faced with anger, Victoria pushed at Quinn's forearm, wanting to step past him and confront Eileen. But his arm was rock-solid. He didn't move.

All his adult life, Quinn had made it a practice to ignore Eileen's frequent outbursts, but her attack on Victoria lit cold rage and pushed him beyond reticence.

"You're wrong, Eileen." His deep voice carried easily in the quiet store where every patron was silent, watching the encounter with open curiosity. "I'd marry Victoria in a heartbeat, if she'd have me. And I'd spend the rest of my life doing everything in my power to make her happy. *Unlike* my father, I'd never be unfaithful to the woman I loved, even if she wasn't the woman I legally married."

A collective gasp rose from the onlookers.

Victoria's heart stopped. He loves me? He wants to marry me? It took a full moment before she realized that Quinn's narrowed, unflinching stare was focused entirely on his stepmother. Victoria glanced at the older woman, shocked at what she saw.

All color leached from Eileen's face, leaving her lips a slash of red against bone-white skin.

"You…that's a terrible thing to say." Her lips trembled. Her hand lifted to press shaking fingers against her mouth.

"I'm sorry, Eileen." Regret tinged Quinn's reply. "I've never denied the things you've said about me. Or Cully. Or our father, because I don't blame you for resenting us. But you've no cause to attack Victoria. She's an innocent bystander in this war you've carried on for years, and I won't let you involve her. Not her."

Not a single person listening misread the threat implicit in his voice.

Not even Eileen.

Visibly shaken, she glanced at Victoria before her gaze returned to Quinn. She drew herself in, her face carefully expressionless except for eyes dark with pain.

"I'm sure I don't know what you mean, Quinn Bowdrie."

With an attempt at her usual haughty stare, her gaze flicked over the silent onlookers. Then she turned on her heel, gathered her shattered composure around her like a cloak and walked from the shop.

Quinn saw the door close on her stiff back before he glanced down at Victoria. Instead of the anger he expected to find, her blue eyes were bemused.

"I'm sorry," he said abruptly. "That was my fault. I should have warned her before to leave you alone."

"It doesn't matter," Victoria dismissed Eileen and focused on more important matters. "Did you mean what you told her?"

"Yes." His response was instant, implacable. "If she ever says anything to you again, or if I hear of her spreading lies about you, I won't let it pass."

Victoria shook her head. "I didn't mean about that. I meant about what you said about loving me and getting married."

Quinn's eyes went hot, naked emotion written on his features.

"Oh, yeah." His voice was husky. "I do. And I'd marry you in a heartbeat, if you'd have me."

"Oh, Quinn." Her smile trembled, her eyes misty as she gazed into his beloved face. "I'd have you."

His big body jerked in reaction, his green eyes blazing with exultation and fierce joy. Then he yanked her against him and swung her off her feet, his mouth claiming hers with swift possession.

Long moments passed before they realized that they had an audience that was clapping, cheering and laughing with delight.

Quinn lifted his head, glanced at the shop's customers, then smiled apologetically at Victoria.

"Sorry, honey. I guess I could have picked a better place to propose."

Victoria laughed and hugged him closer. "I think Colson will just have to get used to seeing us kiss in public because I don't plan to stop."

"At least the town gossips won't have to get the news secondhand," Quinn whispered wryly. "Because Flora Andersen and Elizabeth Price are both standing in the cosmetic section."

"Good," she whispered, smiling sunnily. "Kiss me again so they have a really *good* story to tell. I dare you—just think what this will do for your reputation, Quinn.''

He made a sound that was half groan, half chuckle, and covered her laughing mouth with his.

*   *   *   *   *

Silhouette Special Edition brings you

by SHERRYL WOODS

AND BABY MAKES THREE
The Delacourts of Texas

*Come join the Delacourt family as they all find love—
and parenthood—in the most unexpected ways!*

On sale December 1999:
THE COWBOY AND THE NEW YEAR'S BABY (SE#1291)
During one of the worst blizzards in Texas history, a
stranded Trish Delacourt was about to give birth! Luckily,
sexy Hardy Jones rushed to the rescue. Could the no-strings
bachelor and the new mom turn a precious New Year's
miracle into a labor of *love?*

On sale March 2000:
DYLAN AND THE BABY DOCTOR (SE#1309)
Private detective Dylan Delacourt had closed off part of
his heart and wasn't prepared for what Kelsey James stirred
up when she called on him to locate her missing son.

And don't miss Jeb Delacourt's story coming
to Special Edition in July 2000.

Silhouette®
Where love comes alive™

Available at your favorite retail outlet.

If you enjoyed what you just read,
then we've got an offer you can't resist!

Take 2 bestselling
love stories FREE!
Plus get a FREE surprise gift!

Clip this page and mail it to Silhouette Reader Service™

IN U.S.A.	IN CANADA
3010 Walden Ave.	P.O. Box 609
P.O. Box 1867	Fort Erie, Ontario
Buffalo, N.Y. 14240-1867	L2A 5X3

YES! Please send me 2 free Silhouette Special Edition® novels and my free surprise gift. Then send me 6 brand-new novels every month, which I will receive months before they're available in stores. In the U.S.A., bill me at the bargain price of $3.57 plus 25¢ delivery per book and applicable sales tax, if any*. In Canada, bill me at the bargain price of $3.96 plus 25¢ delivery per book and applicable taxes**. That's the complete price and a savings of over 10% off the cover prices—what a great deal! I understand that accepting the 2 free books and gift places me under no obligation ever to buy any books. I can always return a shipment and cancel at any time. Even if I never buy another book from Silhouette, the 2 free books and gift are mine to keep forever. So why not take us up on our invitation. You'll be glad you did!

235 SEN CNFD
335 SEN CNFE

Name	(PLEASE PRINT)	
Address	Apt.#	
City	State/Prov.	Zip/Postal Code

* Terms and prices subject to change without notice. Sales tax applicable in N.Y.
** Canadian residents will be charged applicable provincial taxes and GST.
   All orders subject to approval. Offer limited to one per household.
   ® are registered trademarks of Harlequin Enterprises Limited.

SPED99   ©1998 Harlequin Enterprises Limited

MONTANA MAVERICKS
Big Sky Brides

Legendary love comes to Whitehorn, Montana,
once more as beloved authors

Christine Rimmer, Jennifer Greene and Cheryl St.John

present three brand-new stories in this exciting anthology!

Meet the Brennan women:
SUZANNA, DIANA and ISABELLE

Strong-willed beauties who find unexpected
love in these irresistible marriage of
covnenience stories.

Don't miss
MONTANA MAVERICKS: BIG SKY BRIDES
On sale in February 2000,
only from Silhouette Books!

Available at your favorite retail outlet.

Celebrate the joy of bringing a baby into the world—
and the power of passionate love—with

A BOUQUET OF BABIES

An anthology containing three delightful stories
from three beloved authors!

THE WAY HOME
The classic tale from *New York Times* bestselling author

LINDA HOWARD

FAMILY BY FATE
A brand-new Maternity Row story by

PAULA DETMER RIGGS

BABY ON HER DOORSTEP
A brand-new Twins on the Doorstep story by

STELLA BAGWELL

Available in April 2000, at your favorite retail outlet.

Silhouette®
Where love comes alive™

SILHOUETTE'S 20TH ANNIVERSARY CONTEST
OFFICIAL RULES
NO PURCHASE NECESSARY TO ENTER

ENTER FOR
A CHANCE TO WIN*
Silhouette's 20ᵗʰ Anniversary Contest

Tell Us Where in the World
You Would Like *Your* Love To Come Alive...
And We'll Send the Lucky Winner There!

Silhouette wants to take you wherever
your happy ending can come true.

Here's how to enter: Tell us, in 100 words or less,
where you want to go to make your love come alive!

In addition to the grand prize, there will be 200
runner-up prizes, collector's-edition book sets
autographed by one of the Silhouette anniversary
authors: **Nora Roberts, Diana Palmer,
Linda Howard** or **Annette Broadrick**.

DON'T MISS YOUR CHANCE TO WIN!
ENTER NOW! No Purchase Necessary

Silhouette®
Where love comes alive™

Name:

Address:

City: State/Province:

Zip/Postal Code:

Mail to Harlequin Books: **In the U.S.**: P.O. Box 9069, Buffalo, NY
14269-9069; **In Canada**: P.O. Box 637, Fort Erie, Ontario, L4A 5X3